Heather Holland Wheaton

You Are Here

HK Publishing   New York

YOU ARE HERE. Copyright ©2010 by Heather Holland Wheaton. All rights reserved. No part of this book may be used or reproduced in any manner whatsoever without written permission except in the case of brief quotations embodied in critical articles and reviews.

For information address HK Publishing, 725 11th Avenue, New York, NY 10019.

This is a work of fiction. Names, characters and incidents are the product of the author's imagination or are used fictitiously. Any resemblance to actual persons, living or dead is entirely coincidental.

Slightly different versions of the following stories originally appeared in *Wet Paint:* "The Perfect Blend of Flexibility and Orderliness," "A Pair," "The Secret Goldfish," and "Jackpot."
"Rain" and "Coats" were originally published in *Every Day Fiction.*

www.heatherhollandwheaton.com

ISBN 0-9720800-2-3
978-0-9720800-2-6

Manufactured in the United States of America

*The author would like to thank
Martin MacKinnon, Elaine Edelman, Sonia Pilcer and Glenn Raucher
for inspiration and support and to the staff at
Perdition for allowing their wonderful bar to be used as an office.*

Contents

Have a Good One.....9
Very Lake Forest.....15
A Bunny's Tale.....19
You Are Here.....25
Doesn't Matter If I Say It or Not.....29
The Perfect Blend of Flexibility and Orderliness.....33
Rain.....37
Lemon and Sugar.....41
Famous Last Words.....45
Close Cover Before Striking.....51
Life Savers.....55
Almost Winter.....59
1-800-CLOSETS.....63
Possibilities.....67
Remote.....71
Neighbors.....77
Coats.....81
A Pair.....85
Because it is Bitter, Because it is My Heart.....87
It's in the Stars.....93
Don't Worry About It.....99
Shelter.....103
Things to Do Today.....107
The Progress of Love.....111
Do You Want to Play Again?.....115
Don't Breathe a Word of This to Anyone.....121
Green Tea.....125
A Day to Remember.....129
Accommodations.....135
Half Empty/Half Full.....137
Inhaler.....145
Metuchen.....149
Fingers Crossed.....151
The Secret Goldfish.....155
Jackpot.....161
Fragaria.....165
Think About It.....169
Change.....173

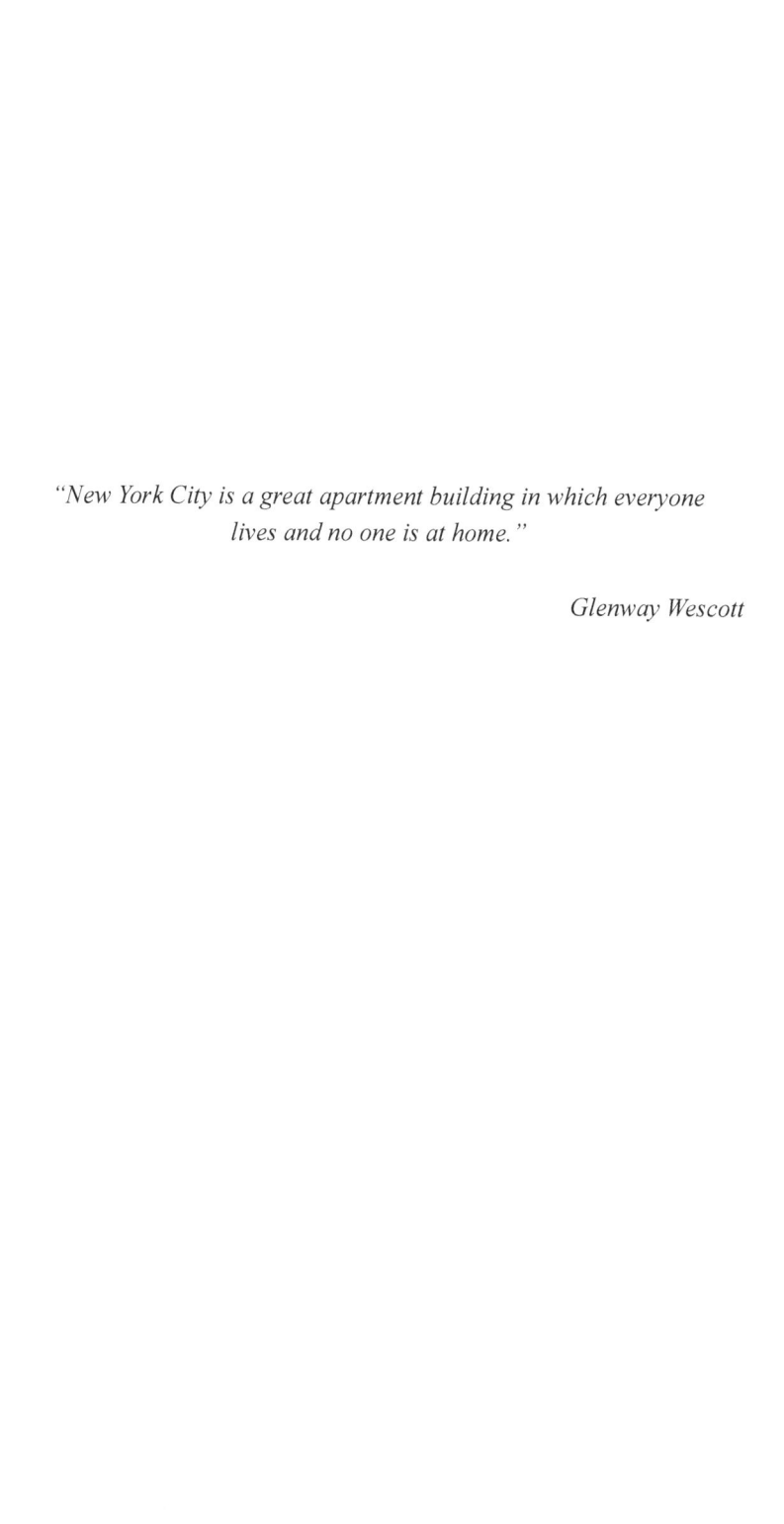

"New York City is a great apartment building in which everyone lives and no one is at home."

Glenway Wescott

Have a Good One

80W80 is an overwrought terra cotta and brick building that lords over the corner of Columbus Avenue and 80th Street. It was originally twelve stories tall, but the current owner, Dewitt Kensington added a penthouse in 1999, making it thirteen.

The goalie for the New York Rangers lives in the penthouse now. His wife drinks too much and cheats on him.

Stanley has seen her stagger home—while the goalie's away, defending the net against penetration by the Penguins or Maple Leafs—with her blouse buttoned up wrong or turned inside out.

Stanley has been the doorman at 80W80 for eighteen years. He's seen it all.

You Are Here

It's Wednesday afternoon and the beginning of his shift. He has a cup of coffee from the deli in his hand and today's *Post* rolled up under his blue-uniformed arm.

The floor in the lobby of 80W80 is marble, but Stanley's rubber-soled shoes don't make a sound as he walks across it and nods at Walter, the morning doorman who's still at the desk.

Walter and Stanley never speak to one another. They just nod.

Stanley waits until Walter has gotten up from the desk and gone into the doormen's locker room before he sits down. The desk is chest-high and topped with marble that matches the floor. On it is a Boerum and Pease logbook where the doormen write down all the comings and goings of the building. It's in military hours:

11:45 Housekeeper to 7E.
11:50 Painters to 10N, new tenant (Gregory Palinuck) will move in Monday.
12:10 MacGregor out w/Buddy, Madison, Mr. Peepers.
13:00 Dry Cleaning: 7N, 10S, 3E, 6N, PH
13:15 MacGregor in w/Buddy, Madison, Mr. Peepers.

Notes: Kaysee O'Brien's car @ 75 81st St. to be moved @ 3PM. Keys in drawer. In Closet: Cohen's baby car seat. Fur coat from Erica Buffett for p/up by Jay Mendel. 2 boxes from Azazel Braunstein for UPS p/up.

The logbook was Stanley's idea. He came up with it when Kensington first bought the building and began to transform it from a rundown piece of real estate that smelled of dead mice into '80W80—A Premiere Residence Boasting Glorious Views of Central Park.'

Gary, the UPS man comes in while Stanley is trying to decipher Walter's sloppy morning entries. "How's it going today, Box Man? How's it going?"

"Not too bad, Door Man," says Gary. "Got three for Azazel. Yarn shipped all the way over from Broadway and 82nd."

Stanley gets up from the desk and retrieves the out-going orders of Azazel's hand-knit sweaters from the closet. "And she's got two for you," he says. "Two for you."

Gary scans the boxes into his DIAD. "Hey, I just saw MacGregor up the block. He's finally leaving Azazel. But he hasn't told her yet."

"I know," Stanley lies. "I know. That's old news. Old news"

"I'm actually surprised he stayed as long as he did."

"It's all about the green card, Box Man. All about the green card."

They both laugh.

"Have a good one, Box Man. Have a good one." Stanley jots the UPS transaction down into the logbook. His handwriting is much neater than Walter's. It's easy to read.

Stanley also has a separate, private notebook with more intimate details about the building. What kind of mood the tenants are in and who they're with, whether they're toting bags from Fairway or sweating from a run in Central Park (two of the tenants—Parker Ross and Ben Bradlee—were in the Marathon last year, although neither one of them finished in under five hours).

Stanley has no plans of writing a tell-all about the building or blackmailing the hockey slut. He keeps the notebook to give him something to do when it's slow. It's also a way to share his day with his wife, Donna. He leaves it out on the kitchen table when he gets home at night so she can read it over breakfast. She likes to know what's happening in the building.

Stanley writes the break-up info about MacGregor and Azazel into the notebook. It's big news and he's actually thinking about calling Donna with it when Homeless Frank shuffles into the lobby.

Frank's wearing three coats, all of them on the verge of disintegrating. His outer coat is black and has what looks like a fresh mustard stain on the lapel. He smells worse than usual.

"How's it going, Frank?" says Stanley, trying not to inhale. "How's it going?"

"I lost my Walkman," says Frank. He coughs dramatically and strokes his beard. "I left it in the park by the tennis courts," he says, "but when I went back for it, it wasn't there. I think somebody found it and kept it."

"That's too bad, Frank. That's too bad." Stanley picks up an envelope with Frank's name on it. In the envelope are five ten-dollar bills that Kensington leaves for Stanley to give to Frank every Wednesday. This too was Stanley's idea.

Frank used to live in the building back when the rent was cheap and the elevators never worked. He wrote jingles for radio spots. Food Emporium, Rockaway Bedding, Duane Reade. He was famous as far as jingle writers go. Then his wife died, suddenly of a blood clot in her brain, and Frank fell apart. He stopped writing ditties about sofa beds and used cars and stopped paying rent. When Kensington bought the building, he had Frank and the other undesirable tenants evicted, legally through the courts. Then their apartments were renovated and leased out at market rate to fine, upstanding people who tip at Christmas.

Fifty dollars a week keeps Frank from hanging out on the corner of Columbus and 80th Street shaking a paper cup of change and telling his story of eviction or singing the Rockaway Bedding song over and over and over again.

Stanley hands Frank the envelope. "Buy yourself a new Walkman. Buy a new one."

"But it had a tape in it of my jingles. My life's work. I can't replace that."

"I'm really sorry," says Stanley. "Really sorry." He means it. "Hey, why don't you put up some flyers in the park? Maybe somebody *did* find it and they just don't know where to return it. You could say on the flyer that they can drop it off here."

Frank smiles. There're only a few teeth left in his mouth. "That's a great idea," he says. "I'm gonna do that. Thanks, Stanley." He salutes him with the envelope of money.

"Anytime, Frank, anytime." Stanley watches him shuffle across the marble floor and waits until he's out the door before he sprays the lobby with lavender air freshener.

Very Lake Forest

Zoë comes out of her bathroom pushing a silver hoop through the hole in her nose.

Her mother's arranging the throw pillows on Zoë's Jennifer Convertible sofa.

"You didn't have to fold that up, Mom," says Zoë. "We're just going to have to pull it out again tonight."

Her mother turns away from the sofa and gestures at the walls of Zoë's living room with a pillow. "I was claustrophobic," she says. "I can't believe you and Alex *both* lived here."

"Well, we did," says Zoë. "And now, until Alex stops drinking and gets his shit together, I live alone. And the apartment is twice as big as it was." She pushes the coffee table back in front of the sofa. The wheels of the table squeak like tiny tortured mice as they move over the floor. "Is that what you're wearing today?" she asks.

Her mother looks down at her outfit; black gabardine slacks and a black crewneck sweater. Knit into the center of the sweater are three large, grinning Jack-o-lanterns. "Don't you like it?"

Zoë picks up her boots from the floor and sits down on the sofa to put them on. "Why don't you wear that blouse you bought at Bloomingdale's yesterday?" She nods at the black silk draped over the top of her mother's suitcase.

"I wore that to *Avenue Q* last night."

"I like that blouse," says Zoë.

Her mother sits down next to her on the sofa. "Don't you like this sweater?" She picks a piece of lint off Zoë's black pants.

"I thought we'd have lunch in SoHo today after we do the Empire," says Zoë. "That blouse from Bloomies, I really like it."

"This is a $300 sweater, Zoë." Her mother stands and walks over to the enormous mirror propped up against the wall—an ornate gold concoction that Zoë found outside her apartment on 46th Street just after she asked Alex to vacate. "This sweater," her mother goes on, "was hand-knit by Azazel Braunstein. An artist that lives right here in New York. This is a one-of-a kind art piece."

"It's lovely." Zoë zips up her boot. "It's just not very SoHo."

"But it's black and expensive and was made in New York," says her mother, still looking in the mirror. "What's more SoHo than that?"

"The Jack-o-lanterns aren't very SoHo. They're very Lake Forest."

Her mother turns from the mirror and puts her hands on her remarkably svelte hips. "Well, having a pierced nose is also very Lake Forest. Every thirteen-year-old there has a pierced nose."

Zoë says nothing.

Her mother turns back to the mirror and begins fussing with her hair. It's cut the same as Zoë's, a modified shag without a bit of gray thanks to Miss Clairol's Chestnut Brown. "And where do you think you learned to dress anyway, young lady? Do you remember those beautiful mother/daughter outfits we had when you were little? Remember the red velvet dresses with the smocking we wore that one Christmas?"

Zoë gets up from the sofa, walks over to the mirror and stands next to her mother.

There's a crack in the middle of the mirror. It slits through Zoë's face just below her silver-hooped nose and intersects her mother's sweater beneath the grinning pumpkins. Below the crack, Zoë and her mother are identical. Black-clad, slim-hipped twins in high-heeled boots.

"I hated those dresses," Zoë says into the reflection of her mother's eyes. "I hated those mother/daughter outfits. I hated dressing like you."

A Bunny's Tale

Benjamin Bradlee and his girlfriend, Fig Vogal live in a one-bedroom apartment in 80W80 with views of the Rose Center for Earth and Space and Central Park. He's an optometrist at MyOptics in Chelsea and she designs eyeglasses for DKNY. Ironically, they met on a blind date and it was love at first sight. That was nine years ago, but they're still not married.

It was Fig's idea for the two of them to dress as Energizer bunnies for a couples costume party at Marshall and Skye's in the East Village. She bought pink sweatpants and sweatshirts and sewed fluffy tails of cotton onto the derrieres, and made special sunglasses with whiskered bunny noses attached.

They're standing in their living room; dressed and ready to go. Mr. Peepers, their black Lab is barking frantically. To Ben, it sounds as if he's laughing at them.

"Quiet, Mr. Peepers," says Ben, but the dog continues to yap. "Stop it. Fig, I feel silly. I'm a respected optometrist. I shouldn't be dressed as a bunny."

"But BB, it's Halloween." She takes a peanut butter-filled Kong from the fridge and tosses it on Mr. Peepers' bed. He stops barking and attacks the Kong with his baloney-colored tongue. "And there'll be a lot of advertising people at the party. They'll think the Energizer thing is funny. Besides." She marches over to him, beating her Energizer drum made from a hatbox. "You look cute. We both look cute." She rubs her bunny nose against his. "We'll be the cutest couple there."

"If you say so," says Ben.

The hosts of the party, Marshall and Skye are dressed as Morticia and Gomez Addams. They do not look silly.

Marshall looks creepy. He always does. Fig worked with him at Ad Inc before she started designing eyeglasses. She said he suffered from a plethora of health issues—acid reflux, chronic back pain, migraines—and kept a cache of amber-bottled prescriptions in the bottom drawer of his desk. They clattered every time he opened it.

Ben shakes his hand. "Thanks for having us."

Marshall nods. His glasses have greasy thumbprints on the lenses.

Skye kisses the air next to Fig and Ben's bunny whiskers. She'd been the one that had fixed the two of them up. She's one of Ben's patients; a former Gap model with a slight astigmatism in her left eye. Ben often wonders how she ended up with someone like Marshall.

"It's good to see you guys," she says. "And you look so cute." She hooks her slim arms through their puffy pink elbows and leads them to a table with a plastic cauldron on it labeled 'Witch's Brew.' "You must try this punch." She ladles out two glasses of brownish liquid. "There's Jack Daniels in it. And tequila and rum and vodka. I found the recipe on the internet."

"Sounds potent," says Fig.

"It is," says Skye. She leaves them to greet more guests; a couple dressed as a post-assassination JFK and Jackie. There's fake blood all over Jackie's dress.

"Well, bottoms up, BB." Fig gulps a mouthful of punch, then turns around and wiggles her cottontail. The pink sweatpants make her hips look even larger than they are.

"Bottoms up." Ben takes a cautious sip.

The party is loud and drunk. House music shrieks through a pair of oversized speakers poised like sentries on opposite sides of the living room. Everyone is young and sexy—even in costume. Nobody else looks silly. Nobody else is dressed as a bunny.

And there aren't a lot of advertising people in attendance. The only person that Fig actually knows is Simon, a copywriter. Ben doesn't know anyone.

Simon doesn't have a date. Instead, he has a blow-up sex doll at his side. They're dressed as Adam and Eve. Felt leaves cover appropriate body parts.

"Did you see who's here?" he asks as Fig hands him a glass of the Witch's Brew. "Right behind you."

Ben and Fig turn to look. On the sofa is Bongo, the lead singer of Shattered Egg. He's not in costume, but the two blonds nestled up on either side of him are wearing devil horns and red teddies.

Ben doesn't listen to Shattered Egg, but he knows who Bongo is. He'd made the cover of the *Post* for three weeks straight when he tried to buy a small, starving country in Africa. His plan was to build a clothing factory there and give all the hungry citizens jobs making T-shirts with clever phrases on them. Then he was busted snorting coke with an underage girl in the bathroom of G.E.L. and the deal fell through.

"He looks much older in real life," whispers Fig, sneaking a photo with her cell.

"He's almost 50," says Simon. "I think he looks pretty good. And obviously he doesn't have to resort to dating blow-up dolls." He squeezes an inflated leaf-covered breast.

"I bet he's a very lonely man," says Fig. "I feel sorry for him."

When they don't win the couple costume contest at midnight, Fig says that it's time to go and the two of them leave the party without saying good night to their hosts.

On the street, it's gotten cold. People in masks and costumes shiver their way home from other parties or from drinking in bars after the parade. The wind eddies bits of discarded costume into tight circles: sequins and feathers, paper crowns, balls of aluminum foil.

Ben takes off his sunglasses and whiskered nose.

"We should have won that contest," says Fig. She stomps down the sidewalk in front of him. There's a glob of Ghoulie Guacamole on her tail.

Skye had made the guacamole ghoulish by using plastic spiders as garnish. She'd told Ben this when she'd offered him some, the bowl deliciously close to her small breasts.

Ben doesn't say anything about the guacamole to Fig; he just watches the green stain bounce along on her tail.

"Our costume was way better than that Sid Vicious and Nancy Spungen," she shouts. "They're such a cliché. And Simon wasn't even a couple—he shouldn't've even been allowed to *enter*."

"Well, in a way," says Ben, "Simon was more of a couple than we are."

Fig stops, turns and puts her hands on her big, bunny hips. "How can you say that? He was with a blow-up doll."

"We're not really wearing a couple costume." Ben hunches his pink shoulders against the wind. "With couple costumes it's supposed to be two different people—usually male and female—that are historically associated with each other. We're just two rabbits."

"So you're saying we're not a couple anymore?"

"I'm saying our costume isn't a couple costume."

"We're not a couple anymore, are we? We're just two people that share an apartment and a dog." She throws her Energizer hatbox/drum into the street and begins walking again. "We've been together for nine years, Ben. Nine years! When you've been together that long you should either get married or break up."

Ben picks up the hatbox and places it on top of a trashcan overflowing with Halloween debris. She is right. They're at that point in their relationship. Still, he just doesn't think that he's ready to get married.

On the other hand, he doesn't want to break up with her either.

Fig stops in front of a group of aliens trying to hail a cab and throws her hand in the air to do the same. She still has her bunny sunglasses on. Ben can't see her eyes, but he knows they're blue with flecks of brown. At times they look gray, sometimes green. He used to tease her that her eyes were like those mood rings from the 1970's.

A cab pulls up and one of the aliens reaches for the door with a webbed hand. Fig butts it away with her hip.

"That's our cab," says the alien. "We were here first."

Fig ignores him and climbs into the back. Ben apologizes, then slides in next to her. He doesn't say anything. Neither does Fig. Finally, the driver asks where they're going.

"Columbus and 80th Street," says Ben. He looks over at Fig who's staring out the window. The cab pulls away from the curb and begins the long journey home.

You Are Here

You Are Here

Norm and his wife, Rose want to get to the opening early, and they aren't exactly sure what part of Manhattan Avenue the gallery is on, so they drive from their home in Flushing Meadows, rather than take the subway.

Norm doesn't say much along the way, but Rose chatters on about the neighborhoods they travel through. "Look at all the new buildings," she keeps saying. "Everything is different. I wouldn't recognize this place if I didn't know where we were."

It turns out that the gallery is easy to find. It's near Java Street in a row of brick warehouses that have been converted into lofts. There's still scaffolding up on the warehouse where the gallery is. A banner stretched across it reads: SoHo Quality Lofts Now Available.

You Are Here

A smaller sign in a gold frame attached to one of the poles near the entrance says:

Norm Schumer: Miniature Watercolors
Gregory Palinuck Gallery, 4th floor
Opening Reception Tonight

"Kind of ironic," says Norm, as he holds the door open for his wife.

"What's ironic?" Rose has on a new dress that she bought special for the occasion. It's covered in bright pink tulips and equally bright yellow pansies. It makes her look like a garden of artificial flowers.

"The fact that I'm a security guard in a warehouse and my paintings are being *shown* in a warehouse." Norm's wearing the suit he bought for their son's wedding, but his shirt and tie are new. "Don't you think that's ironic?" he says and pushes the 'up' button for the elevator.

"I'm sure everything will be fine." Rose grips the handles of her purse with both hands.

The elevator opens up on the 4th floor to a cavernous white-walled space. Tuxedo-ed waiters balancing trays of wine glasses clamor in every direction. Gregory Palinuck stands in the middle of it all with a stainless steel clipboard in his hand.

He waves and makes his way over to the Schumers. "Happy opening night," he says, and shakes Norm's hand. "Is this your wife?" His breath smells of wintergreen.

"Yes," says Norm. "This is Rose. Rose, Greg Palinuck."

"It's a pleasure to meet you. What a beautiful dress."

Rose un-grips her purse and re-centers the belt buckle. "Thank you," she says.

Greg looks at the clipboard. In the center of his forehead is a small, star-shaped scar that Norm never noticed before. "I better give you a tour now," he says, "before the press arrive. It'll be chaos here soon. At least I hope so."

"OK," says Norm.

"I wanted to show your paintings in an environment that would give them room to breathe," says Greg. He leads them to the nearest wall. On it hangs a landscape of a snow-covered mountain in a small gold, curlicue frame. Next to it is a white card that says:

12. *You Are Here*
4 x 6"
watercolor on paper

"See how the large wall makes the small size of the painting have more of an impact?" Greg smiles and the star-shaped scar appears to wink at Norm. "The viewer is shrunk down so he can just climb into the painting and be in this tiny, perfect world." He brings his index finger and thumb a half-inch apart and holds them in front of the painting as if giving the shrunken viewer a boost up from the floor.

"And do you like the title?" he asks. "I gave them all these vague names that evoke a sense of location. 'You Are Here,' 'Arrival,' 'Same Time, Same Place.' What do you think?"

"Great," says Norm.

Rose nods her head.

"And here's a price list." Greg pulls a sheet of paper from the stack on his clipboard and hands it to Norm. Then his jacket begins to vibrate and he takes his cell phone out from his inside pocket. "I've got to take this," he says, looking at the screen. "It's the DJ that was supposed to be here an hour ago. Excuse me a moment." He disappears into the black swirl of waiters and their wine glasses.

Norm and Rose look down on the list of paintings. Number 12, "You are Here" is selling for $7,000. Norm whistles and his wife pulls the list out of his hand.

"$7,000?" she says. "For that? I'd never pay $7,000 for that."

Norm bends close to the painting with his hands clasped behind his back and thinks about the day he painted it in the top drawer of his desk in the warehouse on Orchard Street. The A/C had been on the fritz and the doors to the warehouse were open. It had just rained and the smell of the wet street tumbled into the lobby.

"You're not an art lover," he says, "with $7,000 to spend."

"But there's thirty paintings here and none of them are less than $3,000. Don't you think that's a little high? Didn't you say that Greg had never done this before? Open a gallery and sell art? Didn't you say he's a textile designer? Maybe he doesn't know what he's doing."

Norm takes the price list from Rose. "Yea, but I think he *does* know what he's doing. Look at the frames and the titles and the big white walls. Besides, even if I don't sell a single painting, we're not any worse off. I still have my job. I didn't put any money into this. I didn't even have any dreams about being considered a real artist. I just like to paint instead of doing Sudoku at work. No matter what happens, this is all gravy."

"Gravy?"

"Gravy," says Norm. "And if he does sell a couple of them, we can do some traveling when I retire next year. We can go to places like the places in my paintings."

"Where are these places anyway?" asks his wife. "Where is this mountain? What country is it in?"

Norm shrugs. "I have no idea. But we can look for it. And even if we don't find it, that will be gravy too."

"Gravy," says his wife, and Norm can't tell if the word is a question or an agreement. He puts his arm around her and they stand looking at "You Are Here"—a place that only exists on the 4 x 6 sheet of paper in a gold, curlicue frame.

*Doesn't Matter
If I Say It or Not*

"I need new tennis balls on my walker," says Mrs. Zaplinski. "The ones that are on there now are filthy."

From where she's sitting on the park bench, Jayne can see that the bright yellow balls on the legs of the walker have gotten sooty on the bottoms, most likely from the daily expeditions through Central Park.

Mrs. Zaplinski insists on taking a walk in the park every afternoon at one. Jayne helps her get dressed and lipstick-ed, then maneuvers her and the walker into the elevator and down to the lobby of Mrs. Zaplinski's building where Stanley, the doorman hails a cab to drive them three blocks to the park's entrance.

Jayne pays the cabbie with money that Mrs. Zaplinski has given her. "Don't forget to tip the man," Mrs. Zaplinski always says. Then Jayne clatters the walker from the trunk of the cab, unfolds it and helps Mrs. Zaplinski out of the cab and up onto the curb.

Once they're in the park, Jayne walks patiently beside Mrs. Zaplinski as she takes careful, shuffling steps and comments on the trees and stops to talk to people—out-of-breath joggers; crotchety park gardeners bent over their work; interchangeable blonde mothers clutching Starbucks coffee cups and pushing black Maclaren carriages containing interchangeable babies clutching plastic bottles of pumped breast milk.

By two, they'll reach the Delacorte Theater and they'll sit on a bench so Mrs. Zaplinski can rest, the walker standing at attention beside her, as it is now.

"I'll pick up some new balls from Sports Authority on my way over tomorrow." Jayne pushes a wayward strand of hair behind her ear. It's freshly dyed, with a new shade she found at Ricky's called Torch Crimson. It's very bright, maybe too bright.

"I'll give you some money before you leave this afternoon," says Mrs. Zaplinski. "Remind me. Otherwise, I'll forget." She laughs at this then settles back on the bench. Her feet, shod in Velcro-closure Nikes (also from Sports Authority) dangle an inch off the ground.

Sometimes Jayne wishes she worked for an old woman who was content to sit in her apartment and watch TV or be read to. Jayne loves reading aloud. She loves words; she keeps lists of ones she likes in a notebook. Popsicle, tremor, seethe, zip. She'd planned on being a writer when she first moved to New York but, well, this is what she does instead. She's paid a good salary—Mrs. Zaplinski has gobs of money—her husband invented the Post-it Note, still...

"Maybe what we should do," says Mrs. Zaplinski, "is have two sets of balls. One set for the park—dirty ones and another set, clean ones for my apartment."

"That's an idea." Jayne avoids looking at Mrs. Zaplinski; instead she stares straight ahead through a gap in the trees and sees MacGregor near the Pinetum with three dogs. Mr. Peepers, a seeing-eye-dog school dropout that lives in Mrs. Zaplinski's building; Latte, the caramel-colored poodle from 78th Street and Max, the aging yellow Lab with bad hips that belongs to the New York Rangers goalie.

"You could change the balls in the lobby before we go out and then again when we get back."

"Uh-huh."

MacGregor sees Jayne, waves at her and begins to amble towards the bench.

When he gets to the bench, he'll lift Latte into Mrs. Zaplinski's lap and Latte will wiggle and wag his tail and lick Mrs. Zaplinski's face, his tongue occasionally darting into Mrs. Zaplinski's mouth and Mrs. Zaplinski will tell him that he's the most adorable dog on the Upper Westside. "You're just too cute," she'll say in the same voice she uses with the interchangeable babies in the Maclaren carriages. "So cute I just want to eat you up."

Jayne and MacGregor will then talk about the weather or the neurotic owners that pay MacGregor to walk their dogs or Jayne's latest loser-date that she met on NYLove.com. Every once in awhile, MacGregor will ask Jayne if she wants to have a beer after work. Mrs. Zaplinski does not approve of this because MacGregor is married. He and his wife, Azazel live down the hall from Mrs. Zaplinski in one of the three rent-controlled apartments left in 80W80.

"The notion that men and women can be friends is a load of BS," she'll say to Jayne later on, in the cab or the elevator. "When a man looks at a woman he has only one thing on his mind and that's sex."

Jayne watches MacGregor and the dogs on the path, Max lagging behind, almost dragging his back legs. He's fourteen years old. MacGregor says he really should be put down.

"The squirrels have thick coats this year," says Mrs. Zaplinski. She blows her nose into a pink tissue and checks it for blood. "It's going to be a long, cold winter."

Jayne puts her hands over ears. "Please, don't say that. Please don't."

"Doesn't matter if I say it or not. They have thick coats."

Jayne looks over at the squirrels. There are two of them, fat and furry, jumping in playful circles in a pile of brown oak leaves. All at once, the air smells of winter—fireplaces, wool, fresh snow—even though none of these things are actually around.

Jayne hopes it won't be a cold winter. The walks in the park are seldom canceled because of inclement weather. Blizzards and ice storms, yes. Bitterly cold, no. "The cold keeps you young," Mrs. Zaplinski will say. "Look at me, I'm ninety-three and I'm in much better health than that Madeleine Crane who goes to Florida every winter—and she's only eighty-five."

The squirrels dart up a tree at the sound of Max barking, their tails twitching as if electrocuted and Jayne suddenly hopes that Mrs. Zaplinski will die before the winter comes. Peacefully in her sleep, of course, and Jayne will be forced to get a new job, perhaps at a publishing company where she can wear nice skirts and heels and she'll read manuscripts all day and she'll write a memoir or a novel about her online dating experiences and she'll be spared the icy cold afternoon treks, snow falling gently on the hood of her parka, the bright yellow tennis balls on the walker leading her and Mrs. Zaplinski slowly, slowly, slowly across the barren park.

The Perfect Blend of Flexibility and Orderliness

Tyler Daniels keeps his hand cupped around the mouthpiece of the phone and his eye on the door of Barbara Reid's office. "I figured it out on the subway this morning," he whispers. "I put in about fifty hours a week here in the office, then I still have manuscripts to read. That's another ten hours. I get paid $400 a week, if I do sixty hours; I'm basically making $6.60 an hour—before taxes."

"You might as well work at the Wal-Mart back in Charleston," says Brian.

"No kidding," says Tyler. "Gotta go." He hangs up the phone as Barbara sticks her head out the door.

"Tyler? Can you come in a sec? We need to powwow."

Tyler answers by standing. His tie, a graduation gift from his Aunt Elizabeth flaps to attention; the red stripes align themselves to the horizons of bookshelves along the walls. He walks towards the now-shut door, carefully picking up his feet so he won't create static electricity on the nylon carpet.

He knocks on the door.

"Come in."

Barbara is seated at the glass-topped table that serves as her desk—the 'command center' of Reid & Co. On the wall behind her is a framed blow-up of the jacket of *Anna, I'm Calling Collect,* written by Lowell Farber, Barbara's third husband and number one client.

"Sit down," she says.

Her calendar, a spiral-bound Week-at-a-Glance that's never written in, lies open in front of her. The Post-it Notes of her appointments that Tyler had affixed earlier curl up from the page in neat, canary columns.

Barbara lifts a note from the book. "We need to talk about this new type style on my Post-its. Did something happen to the type-ball?"

"No," says Tyler, "I printed these out on the computer instead of the typewriter."

Barbara squints at the Post-it stuck to the pad of her index finger. "You printed this on the computer?"

Tyler smiles. "Yea, it's from the master copy of your schedule on my hard-drive."

She rubs the front of the Post-it. "I don't feel the indentations of the letters," she says. "And this type style…"

"I used Times Roman, but I could use Courier if you want. That kinda looks like a typewriter."

"Let's do this," says Barbara, sticking the Post-it onto the top of the desk. "You'll re-do my appointments on the typewriter, then make me a few samples of the computer-generated Post-its in Courier. We'll meet on Friday at three and I'll let you know what I think about going forward with this."

"OK."

"And Tyler, in the future, let's not have any surprises with the Post-its. I think it's just terrific that you think outside the box, but things are done around here in a certain way for a reason."

"Yes, Ms. Reid. Of course."

"My assistants have typed out my appointments on Post-its since the first year Post-its came out. Do you know what year that was?"

"No, I honestly don't."

"1980. You weren't even born yet, were you?"

"No, m'am. My parents hadn't even met."

"Typed Post-its give me the perfect blend of flexibility and orderliness," says Barbara.

Tyler smiles. "You should be the company spokesman."

"That's not the point," says Barbara. She stands and smoothes the black skirt that's really too short for a woman her age to wear, even though her legs are in decent shape. The blue veins that run up her calves are fuzzy-ed by sheer black stockings. "The point is," she says, "if it isn't broken, why fix it?"

"It saved me a lot of time this morning. Almost an hour."

"I don't believe that 'saving time' is part of your job description."

"I know, but if I'm more efficient, I can get more done and maybe leave here by eight at night. You see, I kinda need to get a second job to make ends meet."

Barbara looks out the windows facing 57th Street. "Tyler," she says, "how long have you've been in New York City now?"

"Six months."

"Once you've been here a little longer, you'll realize there are some things that are more important than money. Things like experience.

Things like working with authors such as Lowell Farber or reading first drafts of bestsellers like *Sort it Out."*

Tyler says nothing, but his stomach growls. Barbara walks back to her desk and stands behind her black leather chair.

"Having this job is a privilege, Tyler."

"You're right, Ms. Reid."

She sits back down and crosses her vein-y legs before swiveling them under the glass. "Let's get started on re-doing this week's Post-its." She closes the date book and holds it out to him. "I've got one of the computer-generated Post-its for my conference call at ten." She runs her fingers over the edge of the note she'd stuck to her desk. "I'll make the call with that and see how it goes."

"I'll get right on it, Ms. Reid."

"Thank you."

Tyler goes back to his desk, sits down in front of his computer and begins affixing Post-its into columns on an 8 ½ x 11" sheet of paper inked with guidelines. Behind him is the typewriter. A solid, steel behemoth of 1970's technology. Technology that hadn't conceived of 'copy' and 'paste,' 'spell-check' or 'save.' He wheels over to it without getting up from his chair and gets a static electricity shock as he smacks the 'on' button. The typewriter hums, then roars to life, shaking the metal table beneath it.

Rain

It's raining again. Cold, wet sheets of gray are falling in the same steady rhythm they'd been falling in every day for a week.

"Last November we had a heat wave," says Parker, his forehead pressed against the window in Marshall's office, watching the traffic of black umbrella tops on the sidewalk eighteen stories below. "This year, it's cold and wet. Whoever's in charge of weather needs to learn about balance."

"Maybe they should take up yoga," says Marshall, without looking up from his computer.

"Maybe they should," says Parker. He stands upright and leaves a forehead print on the glass. "Maybe whoever's in charge of weather should buy a yoga mat with a Buddha on it. Maybe they should start drinking Chai tea with soy milk."

"Maybe you should get the hell out of my office," says Marshall. "You're giving me a headache."

"Everything gives you a headache," says Parker, but he leaves. He wanders down the carpeted hallway peeking into the offices that are open, looking to see if anyone from the agency is up for lunch. A real lunch, with drinks as an appetizer. He's feeling restless; the rain's getting to him. He'd been Mr. Gung-ho at the beginning of the month, ready to start a dozen new projects that all now seem to be waiting for the sun to shine before he can get back to them.

Everyone in the agency is too busy for lunch. They don't want to go out in that mess, they'll order in and eat at their desks while they work. They tell Parker this as if he should do that too, and he goes back to his office and shuts his door. He puts his feet up on his desk, squeezes a stress ball and watches the endless gray sheets of rain.

A woman appears in the window of the office building on the other side of the street. She's wearing a white blouse that glows in the gloom. She presses her forehead against the glass just as Parker had done in Marshall's office and stands looking down on the street.

She's pretty, thinks Parker. He can see the healthy swell of her breasts beneath the blouse. He can't see her legs or her ass, but he has a feeling that they'd be nice too. He thinks about scribbling a note on a piece of poster board. "Would you like to have lunch?" She looks like the type that would say yes.

He swings his feet off his desk, quickly grabs a piece of foam core and a Sharpie, but when he looks at the window again, she's gone.

"Figures," he says. He resumes his rain-watching position and a black leather desk chair crashes through the window where the woman was standing. It flips over once and plummets, wheels spinning as it falls.

Parker rushes to the window. The chair has already landed on top of a cab by the time he gets there. The driver gets out and waves his arms in wild arcs.

"Holy shit," says Parker.

The woman appears again, framed by the jagged edges of the broken window. She's even prettier without the filter of glass; high, Slavic cheekbones and hair the color of wheat, pulled off her face into a tight French knot. She looks down at the chair and the beginnings of a traffic jam, then looks straight ahead and her eyes meet Parker's.

His eyebrows shoot up to ask what happened and the woman dives with the grace and poise of an Olympic champion over the edges of the shattered window and into the cold river of rain. She lands on the same cab that the chair did, a circle of onlookers already formed, waiting for her without knowing she was coming.

Lemon and Sugar

The three Mexicans in Amsterdam Deli skitter like roaches making eggs sizzle on the grill, paninis ooze cheese in the press and bagels brown in the toaster.

Kwan stands by the register in his green Boar's Head apron patiently listening to a construction worker read a coffee break order from a torn piece of cardboard. When he sees MacGregor, he stops listening and shouts, "Mr. MacGregor! You want tea?"

MacGregor didn't actually come in for tea, but says, "Awright, Kwan," and sticks his hands deep into the pockets of his jeans. "But g'head and take care of this fine fellow first, who is no doubt workin' on that much needed Duane Reade or Chase Manhattan that's going in across the street."

The construction worker glares over his shoulder at MacGregor. A faded "These Colors Don't Run" bumper sticker is stuck on the front of his hardhat.

MacGregor stares at the signs above the grill for sandwiches that the deli's concocted and named for neighborhood icons: "Central Park on Rye," "Shakespeare in the Pita," "The Planetarium Panini." The sandwich named for MacGregor is "The Toasted Scotsman."

Kwan packs the construction worker's cups and foil-wrapped bagels into two bags, rings him up, then makes MacGregor a Taylors of Harrogate tea with one sugar and a slice of lemon.

MacGregor pulls a dollar from his pocket and slides it across the counter. "So I came in to say good-bye to you fucks." He cracks an opening in the plastic lid of his tea.

"You deported?" says Kwan, "You sent back to Scotland?"

MacGregor laughs. "Ah'm just as legal as you, Kwan. In fact, I'm getting' my citizenship next month. I'll be more legal than all ya fucks combined." He laughs again and raises his tea in a mock toast.

The Mexicans look up from cleaning the grill and re-stocking the Snapple, laugh too and start jabbering in Spanish.

"No," says MacGregor. "Ah'm stayin in New York, but I'm moving. Azazel and I are splittin' up."

"You and Misses getting de-vorce?" says Kwan.

"Aye." MacGregor picks up a package of Nemo carrot cake, squeezes the center to test its freshness and tosses it back.

"Me not surprised," says Kwan, shaking his head. "Missus is crazy lady. She not right upstairs."

"Aye," says MacGregor. "Don't I know it."

"Where you moving to?"

"Lexington and 102nd."

"You no walk dogs anymore?"

"No, I'll still walk dogs," says MacGregor, "I'm a dog walker, for fuck's sake, but all my dog clients are on Central Park West or Columbus. I won't be comin' this far west anymore."

The door of the deli opens and Jayne comes in with a frazzled look on her face. She takes care of Mrs. Zaplinski, the old woman who lives down the hall from MacGregor and Azazel. She's wearing tight, low-slung jeans. MacGregor hasn't told her about the divorce.

"Madam wants graham crackers for a snack today," she says, and heads to the back of the deli where the cookies are kept.

"So you no come here anymore?" says Kwan.

"Amsterdam Deli won't be on my path anymore," says MacGregor, lowering his voice so Jayne won't hear. "I've gotta find a new deli. Up where I'm going it's all bodegas owned by Dominicans. No Taylors of Harrogate tea, no Boar's Head ham, no vast selection of imported beers. It's all about Goya products where I'm headed. Goya and big bags of rice."

"No more Mr. MacGregor?"

"'Fraid not."

Jayne returns to the register with a quart of milk and a box of graham crackers. As she takes a crumbled twenty from the pocket of her jeans, a quarter falls to floor. She bends at the waist to pick it up, and MacGregor can see the top of her knickers. They're black.

"You fancy a pint tonight when you're done with Mrs. Z?" he asks.

"Sure," she replies, getting her change. "Dublin House?"

"Ah'll be there round half six."

"See you then." She smiles as she goes out the door, so does Kwan. He nods his head, approving.

"Mr. MacGregor, you good customer," he says. "You spend lotta money here and you make us laugh with your funny accent and your 'fuckin' this' and 'fuckin' that.' I learn the word 'fuck' from you. That very important word in New York City. You teach me English."

"And you taught me Spanish, ya fuckin' Korean fuck. 'Cervesas,' 'dinero,' 'puta.' That'll come in handy in the new bodega place I'll be going to."

"We will miss you," says Kwan.

The Mexicans look up from their Snapple-stocking and floor-sweeping and nod.

"Ah'll miss you too, ya fucks."

"Mr. MacGregor," says Kwan, "I have gift for you." He disappears below the counter, then pops back holding five boxes of Taylors of Harrogate tea. "This for you, Mr. MacGregor."

"Tea?" says MacGregor. "What the fuck I'm going to do with tea? I'm not going to make tea in my new apartment. What do you fuckin' think? I'm going to turn into a crazy tea makin' guy just because I move?"

"No," says Kwan, putting the boxes into a white plastic bag. "You take Taylors of Harrogate to new bodega. Give to them, then buy back with one sugar and lemon. They have tea you like, you buy, you become good customer. We no need Taylors of Harrogate if you not customer. No one buy it but you."

MacGregor considers this and picks up a blue box containing 50 bags of Scottish Breakfast Tea grown in the Brahmaputra Valley of India. He strokes his chin. "Ah like that," he says. "That's a good idea. You're a smart fuck, aren't ya, Kwan? That's very nice of you. Cheers."

Famous Last Words

Olivia Simpson is reclined on her sofa reading *Sort It Out: A Therapist's Approach to Getting Clutter Out of Your Home and Out of Your Life.* It was given to her by its author, Cliff Hobart who lives down the hall. It's fascinating but troubling as well—equating clutter with emotional problems that of course, can be remedied by reading the book and/or attending Cliff's seminars.

    At first, Olivia had been insulted by it, but now, after reading the first chapter, she realizes that she needs help. She puts the book down, face open on her stomach and surveys her living room.

    Her son, Craig is on the computer, his fingers make staccato clicks across the keyboard. The computer is stationed in an antique roll-top desk crammed with yellowing newspaper articles, old bills and office supplies. Next to the desk are stacks of books and magazines; a lacrosse stick and a semi-deflated basketball.

The TV is on and her younger son, Luke is watching a program about sharks. On his lap is a black and white composition notebook where he collects facts about animals. He's sitting on the floor because the two club chairs in the room are filled with discarded jackets, sweatshirts and schoolbags.

According to *Sort It Out*, clutter addiction affects 18% of all US households.

"Hey, Mom," says Craig, without turning away from the computer screen. "Can I use your credit card to buy concert tickets online?"

"What night of the week is the concert?" Olivia picks up the book again and begins Chapter Two, "Where Does Clutter Get You Anyway?" What she should really be reading is a proposal submitted to her about turning The Museum of the City of New York into a destination museum that New Yorkers and tourists actually long to go to.

"It's on a Friday night," says Craig.

"Where is it?"

"Madison Square Garden."

"And who's playing?"

"Shattered Egg."

"Sweetie, you know how I feel about their lead singer."

"Bongo?"

"Yea, Bongo. I don't agree with his politics." She marks her place in *Sort It Out* by folding down a corner of the page. She then closes the book, walks over to the desk and kisses the top of Craig's head.

"But Mom, Bongo's trying to help people. He wants to save the world."

"By snorting coke with underage girls?"

"What about the New York Dolls?" Craig tilts his head so he's looking up at her. There's a constellation of tiny pimples mapped out on his forehead. "You listened to them when you were my age," he says, "and they did drugs all the time. Didn't some of them die from drug overdoses?"

"Good point," says Olivia.

Craig's always making good points. He could be a lawyer when he grows up. Thankfully, he wants to be an architect. Olivia kisses his head again and picks up the museum proposal; it's bound in fake brown leather. "But Johnny Thunders never claimed to be the Word Made Flesh," she says, "and the Dolls never tried to save anything."

"Didn't The New York Dolls dress up in ladies clothes?" asks Luke. "Didn't they wear lipstick and eye shadow?"

"Yes, they did, Honey." Olivia sits down on sofa with the proposal. "And if Bongo really wanted to help the starving in Africa, he'd sell his fifteen million dollar apartment in the Beresford. Fifteen million would buy a lot of food."

"C'mon Mom," says Craig. "Can't I just go and just listen to their music? I promise not to be influenced by Bongo's politics or do lines of coke with underage girls. I won't even buy a T-shirt."

Olivia cocks her head and thinks about the battles she'd had with her parents about music. They'd been Dylan fans. They never 'got' The Dolls or The Cramps or Iggy and the Stooges. That of course, had been part of the appeal. Nobody wants to like the same music that your parents like when you're thirteen.

"How much are tickets?" she asks.

"$125 plus the Ticketmaster charge."

"Are you kidding? $125 each?"

"It's a benefit. Proceeds go to—."

"Don't tell me. I don't want to know. My wallet's in my bag on the chair. Use the Amex."

"You're the coolest, Mom. And I'll pay you back when I'm old enough to get a job."

"Famous last words," says Olivia. "Just take care of me when I'm old. Visit me in the nursing home."

"Can I go to Shattered Egg with Craig?" says Luke.

"No way. I'm taking Jill." Craig's hand is deep inside Olivia's bag, rummaging for her wallet. "When was the last time you cleaned this out?" he says. "Look at this." He pulls out a pacifier. "Is this your Binky, Luke?"

"No," says Luke. "Binkies are for babies. Shut up."

"I don't know where that came from." Olivia opens the proposal and begins reading. She likes the idea of a Museum Makeover. At times, she's embarrassed to be a curator in a museum that's only visited by school groups and retired tour guides. Even Craig and Luke find the place dull. They'd be much happier if she worked at the Museum of Natural History.

After a few moments more of keyboard clicking, Craig announces that the ticket transaction is complete. "Computer's all yours," he says to Luke. "I got to get to soccer practice."

Luke swivels into the computer chair as Craig swivels out and bolts down the hallway to their bedroom.

"Turn off the TV if you're not watching it, Luke," says Olivia.

"I'm still listening to it," he says. "I'm multi-tasking."

"'Multi-tasking'?" Olivia smirks. "Is that a word you learned at school?"

"No, from you."

Luke returns with his skateboard under one arm and his soccer bag slung over his shoulder. His iPod is tucked into the front pocket of his jeans; one of the earbuds is already in place, the other dangles at his chest. He sits down on the sofa next to Olivia and hands her a CD. "Listen to this, Mom. I think you'll like it."

On the cover is Bongo, naked from the waist up, his arms stretched out messiah-like, embracing the world. Olivia turns the CD over to read the names of the songs but the print is too small. "Put it in my bag," she says. "I'll listen to it tomorrow at work."

"Famous last words. If I put in that bag, it will never be seen again."

"I promise I'll listen to it *and* clean out my bag, OK?"

"OK. I'll be home around eight." Craig inserts the second earbud and turns on the iPod.

Olivia pulls the wire out of his ear. "Only one earbud while you're skateboarding in traffic. You can't listen to music if you're dead."

"How do you really know that?" He smiles broadly, showing the chipped front tooth that needs to be fixed.

"I'm serious."

"OK."

But like all kids, even ones with the coolest moms, Craig disobeys. He keeps both earbuds in while he skates down Columbus Avenue. The iPod fills his ears with hypnotic beats; ones that change with every generation, but are essentially the same boom-ta-bumph rhythms of rebellion that make you feel alive and a part of everything.

He hears nothing but the music. He doesn't hear the jackhammers attacking the concrete on 77th or the ranting of the homeless man in front of Nancy's Wines. He doesn't hear the horn of the cab speeding through a red light at 74th Street or the screech of its brakes as the driver tries to stop or the sickening crunch of his own bones as the cab skids into him.

Close Cover Before Striking

When Valerie moved out of her parents' house in Long Island, she took a few old lamps, some mismatched dishes, a silver cigarette box and an enormous glass ashtray.

In the '60's, Valerie's parents always kept the box filled with cigarettes even though neither one of them smoked. People did that kind of thing back then. You kept cigarettes on hand even if you didn't smoke for your friends and guests that did. When her parents 'had company,' her mother would offer them a cigarette from the box and her father would light it with a heavy matching lighter that sat next to the box and the ashtray on the cocktail table.

Valerie smokes, but she keeps her cigarettes in the package that they come in and she lights them absently with whatever's handy. She doesn't notice that she's smoking unless she has to go somewhere else to do it. On the 34th Street side of Macy's if she's at work or on the sidewalk if she's at a bar. And she used to smoke on the fire escape when she was living with her now ex-boyfriend, Howard Manspeaker.

"I couldn't just smoke out the window," she says to Tim, who she's just met while smoking outside Dive 75. She whispers because there's a sign requesting patrons of the bar to be considerate of the neighbors while they're smoking or using cell phones. "I had to climb out onto the fire escape," she says. "Even if we'd just had sex. And I was paying half the rent."

"That must've sucked." Tim flicks his thumb on the edge of his filter. He's wearing a fanny pack. It bulges like a first trimester pregnancy above his crotch. His hair is just this side of being a mullet. "Is that why you broke up with him?" he asks.

"No." Valerie shakes her head and shivers as a swirl of dead leaves shimmies down the sidewalk. She should've put on her jacket before coming out here. "There was more to it than that."

She doesn't tell Tim that Howard broke up with *her*, legally changed his name to Bongo and is now one of the most famous musicians in the world. She also doesn't say that the most annoying thing about the smoking ban in New York City bars is the smoking-centric conversations she's forced to have with other smokers while standing outside having a cigarette; the superficial bonding with people that she'd probably never speak to otherwise.

After taking a final drag, she throws her cigarette in the street. "I'm freezing," she says to Tim. "I'm going inside."

"Me too." He follows her.

Valerie kept business cards in the silver cigarette box back when she first moved to the city. People in the fashion industry that might someday be influential in her dream of being a famous designer. After three years of nothing, she threw them out.

Then, when she'd lived with Howard/Bongo, she collected the thin slips of paper that came out of her fortune cookies. Vague predictions that she always interpreted as a happy future together. She tossed her change in the un-used ashtray. There was nearly thirty dollars in pennies, nickels, dimes and quarters when he left.

Now Valerie keeps condoms in the box. It sits on the nightstand next to her bed. The ashtray is there as well. She balances it on Tim's belly after they have sex and they smoke. Long, indulgent clouds that they blow out through puckered lips at the ceiling.

Tim puts the used condom in the ashtray, but there's still plenty of room to flick their ashes and crush out their butts.

Life Savers

The first place Greg looks for the check is in the pencil drawer of his desk. He vaguely remembers putting it there after he'd made the sale; after he'd bowed to Mr. Akita so many times his back began to ache, trying to look businessman-cool, as if selling $25,000 worth of art was an everyday occurrence.

In the tray of the pencil drawer are a handful of Italian paperclips shaped like spirals, two Waterman pens and a roll of wintergreen Life Savers. The Life Savers are open; Greg had popped one in his mouth when Mr. Akita had come in so he wouldn't offend him with coffee breath. A thin strip of foil from the roll curls upwards.

Greg wheels back his desk chair and peers all the way into the drawer. The only thing there is a package of Post-it Notes. No check.

It's quarter past three. If he can get to the bank by four and deposit the check, it'll clear by Wednesday. $25,000 in the account will keep the gallery's rent check from bouncing. He'll also be able to pay the Amex and Verizon bills in full for the first time since the gallery opened.

The phone on his desk rings. It's a full-on proper office phone with an intercom and buttons for six lines even though there's only one. He lifts up the entire phone as he answers it to see if the check has slid under it. "Gregory Palinuck Gallery."

"I got the part. I'm going to be on Broadway!"

"Candace?" He puts the body of the phone back and scans the top of his desk. "Congratulations. I knew you'd get it." He picks up a copy of *Art in America* and fans through it, hoping the check will slip out, but the pages yield nothing except subscription cards that dive-bomb to the floor. Greg tosses the magazine into his empty IN box; it's stainless steel. He'd bought it in the MoMA gift shop to help him be more organized. One hundred and fifty bucks.

"They're going to cut my hair," says Candace, "and bleach it blonde. I have to look like a trashy waitress. I chew gum the entire time I'm on stage."

"Uh-huh."

"You know, it's funny. I don't even like Supertramp and here I am performing their songs on Broadway."

"That *is* funny." Next to Greg's IN box is a rubber-banded stack of postcards leftover from the gallery's opening. He'd had them printed through his friend, Mickey who specializes in printing for art galleries. Greg had thought that Mickey would've given him a break on the price; they've been friends since college. He hadn't.

They were great postcards though and it had been a successful opening. The gallery had gotten amazing press. And not just art mags. *New York*, *Vanity Fair*—even the *Post* had done something on it. The big draw was that the artist, Norm Schumer was a security guard in a warehouse when Greg had 'discovered' him. Greg has made quite a few sales since, but somehow, the cash flow was still very fucked up.

"I think you should take me out to dinner to celebrate," says Candace.

"Definitely." Greg looks under the postcards for the check, then opens the pencil drawer again. This time feeling around in the back of the drawer, his sweaty palm squeaks against the wood. Nothing.

"How 'bout G.E.L.? Everybody's raving about it."

"Yea, yea." Greg looks back down at the open pencil drawer, at the Italian paperclips, the pens and the Life Savers. Wintergreen is spelled 'Wint-O-Green.' The 'o' is thick and white, a real circle, mirroring the shape of the candy.

When Greg had been a kid, his father had brought home a roll of wintergreen Life Savers one day and had told Greg that if he chewed them in a dark room, blue sparks would fly about his mouth.

"No other flavor of Life Saver does this," he'd said. "Only wintergreen."

His father had then led him into the bathroom, turned off the light and laid a Life Saver communion-like onto Greg's tongue. "Try it," he'd said.

Greg had looked into the mirror of the dark bathroom and crunched down on the Life Saver with his molars. Bright pinpricks of blue light crackled in his mouth for a split-second then disappeared. He bit down again, more sparks, like fireflies, right there in his mouth. He chewed and watched, while his father stood behind him, monologue-ing what made this happen. Colliding electrons, excited nitrogen molecules, ultraviolet light. His father had turned everything into a lesson on physics or mathematics.

Greg closes the pencil drawer, bends over in his chair and scans the floor for the check.

"I read something somewhere," says Candace, "the owners of G.E.L.—I can't remember their names, they had this idea to open a restaurant with a menu based on gelatin products. They just did it and— boom! Now it's *the* restaurant to go to."

"Uhuh." He rummages through the wastebasket, also from MoMA and also stainless steel. Inside are his empty Starbucks cup and several pieces of crumpled up paper. The paper is white, not check-blue.

"So about seven then?" says Candace. "Pick me up in a cab?"

"You mean tonight?" Greg sits upright. "I don't know about that."

"But I just got a part in a Broadway show."

He opens the pencil drawer again. "Candace, I really can't talk right now. I made a sale this morning. To the CEO of Sony Japan. $25,000. I don't remember where I put the check."

"You need to hire an assistant," says Candace. "Or an accountant. Or someone to help you out."

"I don't have the time or the money to do that."

"But you're losing time and money by not having one."

"I know, I know. It's a vicious cycle," says Greg. "Listen, I've got to get off the phone and find this check. I'll talk to you later, OK? I'm just too stressed to think about anything else right now."

After he hangs up, Greg stares at the Life Savers, then picks up the roll and goes into the gallery's bathroom without turning on the lights. There's no window, it's completely dark, as if the bathroom had been filled up with black ink.

Greg flips three Life Savers into his mouth, looks at the mirror and bites down hard with his molars. He chews and watches the blue sparks fly like pinpricks of neon, like little electric jewels, like tiny bits of possibility.

Almost Winter

Madeleine Crane wakes to the sounds of two pigeons mating on her window ledge. There's much cooing and wing-flapping. Occasionally one of the bodies slams against the glass.

Her four white cats Eeny, Meany, Miney and Mo are asleep on the bed next to her, oblivious to the noise. They gave up pigeon hunting when they were still kittens and learned that they'd never get outside to catch them. Better to spend their time stalking one another or batting around a catnip-filled mouse.

During the night, Madeleine's flannel nightgown has twisted up and around her waist, exposing the silver-gray triangle of her pubic hair. The nightgown falls gracefully to her ankles as she gets out of bed and makes her way to the kitchen.

You Are Here

The cats also rise and one-by-one, leap off the bed and follow.

Madeleine moves slowly, but with what she calls 'New York purposefulness and determination,' her shoulders squared, her back as straight as possible. She considers herself ancient—she's eighty-five, but doesn't look it or feel it most of the time.

As she fills the teakettle with water, Madeleine looks out the window above her sink. The sun is just beginning to come up over the trees in Central Park. They're nearly bare; a few brown leaves cling to the branches and writhe fitfully in the wind. It's almost winter, a season she's despised since childhood.

At the end of the month, she'll go visit her niece, Natalie, in Palm Beach as she does every year, hiding from the cold, bleak days and bitter, frigid nights. She'll sit in the warm sun and chat with the other old ladies who live in Natalie's building. They'll swim in the heated pool—long, lazy laps of the sidestroke, their faces never coming in contact with the water.

When Madeleine returns to New York in March, she'll be tanned and radiant. Mrs. Zaplinski, her next-door neighbor will comment about how damaging the sun is, her own skin as gray as the winter she just suffered through.

Mo jumps up on the counter and swats at the water coming out of the faucet.

"Are you hungry, Mo-Mo?" says Madeleine and shoos him away. "I'll get you your breakfast in a moment."

She puts the kettle on to boil, then takes four tins of Blue Spa Select Feline Cuisine out of the cupboard. Savory Salmon for Eeny, Hairball Control Formula for Meany, Chicken for Miney and Mo. The cats each have their own white ceramic dish with their name painted across it in red, specially made at Pet Bowl on Amsterdam Avenue.

After she feeds the cats, Madeleine sits down at the kitchen table with her tea, and looks at the list of things she needs to do before her trip.

It's written on notepaper bordered by paw prints:

Have mail forwarded
Talk to Azazel about looking after the cats
Order 3 months of cat food to be delivered
Gift for Natalie
Get prescriptions refilled

Today she'll go shopping and look for something to bring Natalie. Maybe a piece of jewelry, something silver and funky. She'll go to Bergdorf's.

Like Madeleine, Natalie has never married, although she still has hopes. She thinks there is one special man out there waiting for her, the way she's waiting for him. Natalie doesn't want to end up alone.

Madeleine likes to remind her that after a certain age, all women end up alone, whether it's from divorce or death. At least Madeleine was used to it.

"Alone, except for my cats," she says.

Meany jumps up into her lap and meows. He's actually the friendliest despite his name. Madeleine scratches his head; his fur is baby-blanket soft beneath her fingers. "Who's the pretty kitty?"

Leaving them for three months will be tough, it always is, but there's no alternative. Madeleine cannot possibly bare the thought of spending the winter in New York and the cats cannot go to Florida with her. Natalie is allergic to cats—and to shellfish and peanuts.

Natalie is also rather frumpy. Her sad, but smoky eyes are always hidden behind thick, tortoiseshell glasses; her dark, limp hair always pulled back in a barrette. She doesn't fit in with the thin, beautiful people of Palm Beach and Madeleine often wonders if Natalie would do better in New York where glasses and dark hair are considered acceptable if not alluring. She'd at least get a shot at having a love affair with a divorced accountant or optometrist. Natalie's such a sweet, smart young woman—she deserves a little romance.

The cats follow Madeleine into the bathroom. They watch her slip her nightgown over her head and turn on the water for her shower. Meany sits on top of the wicker hamper and licks his paws.

Madeleine's bathtub is a deep, claw-footed one. The enamel is scratched and worn from years of use. There's a long teardrop-shaped rust stain coming up from the drain.

She steps into the tub carefully. While she showers, she thinks of other things she needs to buy before she leaves. Some new clothes, a few Lilly Pulitzers in bright pinks and greens, Lilly's signature hidden in the pattern of the fabric—in the wings of a butterfly or the leaves of a palm tree.

She should also pick up a few gifts for the cats, some new toys to play with in her absence, toys with feathers and bells and ones that squeak when pounced on.

That might have to wait for another day.

She doesn't see Meany until she's actually getting out of the tub. He's sleeping on the bathmat, curled up into a furry white 'c.' To avoid stepping on him, she shifts her weight and as she does so, she slips. When she grabs the shower curtain to catch herself, it rips from the rings one-by-one and Madeleine is falling. The cats watch her fall, their eyes blink helplessly, their long tails twitch in the air.

1-800-CLOSETS

Somehow, Candace has accumulated a total of eighty-nine black skirts.

"Truly amazing," says Henry, the consultant from Closet Cases. He has just counted and sorted the skirts into three separate piles on Candace's bed.

One pile contains fifteen black skirts that Candace wears on a regular basis; another pile is a half dozen she wears once in awhile. The third is a large, black mound that she's never worn at all—most with the tags still attached. They'll be donated to Housing Works.

Henry peers into the mish-mash of blouses, jackets and shoes that remain in Candace's closet. He reminds Candace of a guy she'd worked with on an episode of *Law and Order*; he has the same solid, square jaw that always gets an actor cast as either a cop or a criminal. In his hand is a clipboard holding a small stack of papers. On the back it says, "Closet Cases, NY's Holistic Approach to Home Organization."

"We can add another pole," he says, scribbling onto the clipboard with a red pen that also advertises the company. "And install shelves up here." He points to the top of her closet and clicks the pen twice with his thumb. "We'll put a row of hooks on the insides of the doors for belts and accessories, units for shoes on the bottom..." He clicks the pen again and underlines something on the clipboard. "That's if you get the Regular Package, but I think you're a good candidate for the Deluxe."

"How much is the Deluxe?" says Candace. She sits down on a small patch of the bed not covered in black skirts.

"With the Deluxe, you'll get the same Closet Makeover—the poles, the hooks, the shoe units..." Henry picks up his Closet Cases tote bag from the floor. "But you'll also receive a copy of the best-selling book *Sort It Out* by Closet Cases founder Cliff Hobart." Henry produces the book from the bag and hands it to Candace. "*And* you'll get a voucher for a free therapy session with him. That alone is a $500 value."

"Therapy session?" says Candace, flipping through the book, but not really looking at it. "I don't need therapy."

"But you're obviously a shopaholic."

Candace laughs. "Well, I'm guilty of that," she says, throwing her hands in the air, surrendering.

"It's not funny," says Henry, his face grim, the solid criminal/cop jaw clenched like a fist. "Shopping too much is a type of Clutter Hoarding and that's usually a sign of emotional issues."

"What're you talking about?"

"It means you have a void in your life that you're trying to fill." Henry tucks the clipboard under his arm and the pen into his pocket. "You feel there's something missing, so you try to fill that void by shopping for things you don't need. That's how you ended up with eighty-nine black skirts."

"No, you've got it all wrong," says Candace. "There's no void in my life. Nothing's missing. My life is perfect. I'm starring in a musical on Broadway, I have an amazing boyfriend who absolutely adores me, I have this great apartment—I have everything."

"Perhaps it goes back to your childhood," says Henry.

"I had a wonderful childhood," Candace lies. "A textbook-perfect upbringing." She picks up a black skirt that she doesn't remember owning or even buying. The hem has red sequined roses sewn on to it. *It's hideous. Like the sort of thing Mom used to wear when she was trying to look 'classy.'* She tosses it back onto the pile to be donated. "Besides," she says, "I don't think my childhood is any of your business."

"It *is* my business," says Henry. "You called Closet Cases because you need help organizing this mess and I'm telling you—as a Trained Closet Professional—that the first step is admitting that you have a problem."

"Can I just get the Regular Package? The poles, the hooks and the units for my shoes." Candace pulls another black skirt from the donation pile. Short wool with dozens of tight, slim pleats. She remembers buying this one. A rainy November afternoon at Century 21. There was that thrill of finding it on the rack, half-off the hanger. Originally $395, marked down to $189.99.

Henry takes the pen back out of his pocket and begins to click it as he speaks. "Sure—click—you can—click—get the Regular Package—click—and we'll purge your closet—click—and get everything neat—click—and tidy—click—but in six months—click—it's going to end up—click—looking the same—click—as it does now—click—unless—click—you address—click—your—click—addiction. Click. Click. Click."

Candace spreads the pleated black skirt out over her lap and strokes it. *It's really cute.* She should wear it someday. "Look, it's a pretty benign addiction," she says. "I think I'll just get the Regular Package."

Henry lifts the donation pile of skirts off the bed, drops them on the floor and sits down next to her. "I hate to use a bad pun," he says, flipping through the papers on his clipboard to a blank sheet. "But you're skirting this issue here." He writes ADDICTION in the center of the paper. "Having an addiction to shopping is the same as having an addiction to heroin or gambling or sex."

His letters are large, jagged and accusing. Candace sees pale dope fiends shooting up in dark alleys, toupee-ed men in plaid sport coats cheering on horses circling a dusty race track and sleazy politicians getting caught with high-priced hookers from Upper Eastside escort agencies. She also sees her own monthly credit card bills and their horrendous interest charges.

"But Closet Cases is here to help." Henry puts his arm around Candace's shoulder and gives her a reassuring squeeze. His chiseled-cop jaw is just inches away from her face. "It helped me."

"Really?"

"Really. My problem was paper clutter. My apartment was overrun with it. Boxes filled with old tax returns and cancelled checks. Piles of catalogs that I knew I'd never order from. Why? I was abused by my uncle until I was thirteen and I was trying to build a wall of paper to protect myself."

"Oh," says Candace. "I'm sorry."

"No, no. I've battled my demons and I'm free of clutter—it feels great. And the best part is now I get to help people with the same clutter issues." He lays his hand over Candace's; it's solid and square like his jaw. "People like you," he says softly.

"I don't know," she says. "It just all seems a little—a little outrageous."

"So is owning eighty-nine black skirts."

Candace stands up and drapes the pleated skirt over her arm. "I'll think about it," she says. "I'll call and let you know."

Possibilities

Azazel is sitting at the kitchen table, finishing a sweater with a cat's face on it. Cat sweaters sell very well on her website, particularly in the Midwest. She clips the last piece of yarn with a small pair of scissors that can be folded up and taken anywhere, although the only place she ever knits is here in the kitchen.

When she looks up from her work, she notices a door on the wall next to the sink that she's never seen before.

How could I have never noticed a door in my kitchen before? She's lived in the apartment for over thirty years. How many hundreds—thousands—of times has she sat here at the kitchen table, but never seen it?

After staring at it for a few moments, she gets up from the table and walks over to it. Her slippers shuffle-slap against the linoleum. The door is painted eggshell-white like the walls and there's a doorknob on it made of cut-glass.

She takes a breath, reaches out and places her hand on the knob. It's real and solid; she can feel the cool, smooth planes of each facet against her palm. It turns easily and the door opens with a swollen-wood pop.

Behind the door is a room slightly smaller than her bedroom. It's empty and smells of bug spray. The walls are dingy beige and dotted with nail holes, perhaps they'd been white once, but now they're the color of band-aids. On one wall is a window looking out at the apartment building on the other side of 80th Street.

Azazel lets out a nervous laugh and walks into the middle of the room, taking it all in and leaving a trail of slipper-prints on the dusty floor. A room in her apartment that she hadn't known about. *How is that possible in Manhattan?*

She begins to think of all the things she can do with the room. If she put up shelves, she could move her yarn and needles and all the UPS supplies out of the kitchen. Get a desk for her laptop and be more organized and business-like about Knitopia.com. Maybe start shipping orders out the same week that they come in.

On the other hand, I could rent the room out. Not that she needs the money. Her apartment is one of three rent controls left in the building. Selling just four sweaters a month pays for it, but it'd be good to have some company.

The apartment's felt hollow since MacGregor moved out. Having a tenant would be nice. Someone to say good morning to, someone to sit across the kitchen table from her and share an order of Chinese delivery. Maybe a philosophy student from Columbia.

Either way, I'll have to have the room painted first. Eggshell white, like the rest of the apartment. The same white Dewitt Kensington uses to make everything look bigger and cleaner. *I'll call him first thing tomorrow morning.*

She walks over to the window and tries to open it, to get the smell of bug spray out. It's sickly-sweet, almost medicinal and beginning to nauseate her, but the window's been painted shut.

I'll have him fix that too. She looks out at the building across the street, there's a row of terra cotta Indian heads along the top floor. *But then again,* she thinks, *if Dewitt finds out about this room, he'll raise my rent. My lease will be null and void.*

Azazel sits down on the sill with her back to the window.

But how could he not know about it already? He owns the building after all. But my lease is for a one-bedroom.

Her hands begin to shake; her pulse throbs in blue bumps at her wrists. Sweat pops up on her forehead. She presses her fingers against her temples, hoping to hold in what's left of her sanity.

It isn't just the room. There've been other things, like being afraid to step on manhole covers and not being able to look at the color orange anymore. Something about it puts her teeth on edge. She had to discontinue the line of pumpkin sweaters on her website.

And sometimes she sees blue flashes of light from the corner of her eye. Krystal, Azazel's spiritual liaison, says the flashes are bits of negative psychic energy; her chakras have been off-kilter since MacGregor left. Krystal advises taking baths with tansy oil to remedy this. It hasn't helped.

And then there're the voices. Throaty murmurs that sound like Latin. Azazel hasn't told Krystal about the voices, she hasn't told anybody about them. Hearing voices is for crazy people.

And Azazel isn't crazy.

Neurotic, heartbroken, emotionally wrought, yes. Crazy, no. She couldn't be crazy.

Nor could she be mad, insane or nuts. That was for a higher level of creative people, for geniuses. Artists went mad and painted masterpieces, insane poets won Pulitzers for their work; rock stars lost their minds and had #1 hits.

But Azazel is a fifty-year-old Jewish woman who knits overpriced sweaters for a living. The term for her would be 'mentally ill.' Sterile, clinical. Nothing great to show for it.

"I am mentally ill," she says aloud. It suddenly feels OK to be talking to herself. "So what do I do about it?" She pushes the sweat off her forehead and into her gray wooly hair. "Do I check into Bellevue and knit myself a strait jacket? Do I swallow a handful of pills and leave a note blaming it all on my mother? Or maybe I should buy a gun and start shooting people at Fairway?"

But Azazel doesn't want to do any of that.

"I'm still *so* normal," she wails. "I pay my rent, I talk to my friends on the phone, I visit my sister in Brooklyn—I do all the normal things that normal people do. But I hear voices and sit in dusty rooms that don't actually exist."

A cool breeze swirls into the room. Azazel lifts her hot face to it. Maybe she should just go back in the kitchen and have a cup of tea. Or call Krystal and tell her about the voices and the room. Maybe it's just part of her off-kilter charkas.

She closes her eyes, rubs her temples and hears the door of the room slam shut.

The slam rattles the glass in the windowpane; it vibrates against Azazel's back. She leaps from the sill, hurries to the door and grabs the knob. It doesn't turn. She pulls at it, jiggles it, and the knob comes off in her hand.

The smell of bug spray is overpowering. Sour bile and chunks of the tuna on rye that she had for lunch burn halfway up her throat.

She rushes back to the window. It still won't open. Sweat rivers down her forehead, stinging her eyes. She begins to hit the window with the heels of her palms. She bangs her hands against it until the glass shatters.

Remote

On a sunny day in September, Alex's wife, Zoë ordered him out of their apartment in Hell's Kitchen.

"Don't come back until you've stopped drinking," she'd said, depositing a duffle bag of his clothes outside the door. "And you've gotten your shit together."

He crashed for a while on his buddy, Simon's lumpy pullout sofa in Washington Heights until Simon asked him to vacate. His cousin, Emily was moving to the city and needed a place to stay.

"Sorry," Simon had said. "But blood is thicker than Budweiser. You understand."

So Alex rents a room in a house way out in Queens owned by a man named Leon Hudson. The room is small; furnished by a narrow twin bed and a dresser with faded stickers of dinosaurs stuck on the drawers. The walls are painted a color that Alex can only describe as 'Post-it Note Yellow,' but the room is cheap and has a window that looks out onto the World's Fairground in Corona Park.

Five nights a week, Leon drives a cross-town bus in Manhattan and he tells Alex that he's welcome to sit in the living room and watch TV while he's at work.

"I've got Super-Cable," says Leon. "Over four hundred channels. And this chair's got heat and massage." He pats the top of the leather La-Z-Boy proudly—like a child that's gotten A's on his report card. "And you can adjust it to any position. It's pure comfort."

Alex never watched TV when he lived with Zoë—they hadn't owned one. She's a teacher at the Metropolitan Montessori School and thinks TV is addling the collective mind of America. She read at night after work and toiled over lesson plans. Alex went out with friends (who all had important, exciting careers in advertising or the music industry) and drank until he got depressed about his own job at a tiny bookstore in Penn Station.

"It's a true Dante's hell-hole where I work," he'd slur dramatically. "A world of rushing and waiting. I'm in the very center of New York City, but so far removed from it—sometimes I never see the light of day."

But once Alex moves to Queens; he doesn't feel like going out with the guys. He doesn't want any conversation. He doesn't feel like being social.

And it's a nice escape, the TV. There's no need for Alex to think at all, he can just exist, cocooned in the La-Z-Boy that reclines and vibrates; the remote control snug in his hand.

He begins buying *TV Guide* and using a yellow marker, he highlights programs that look interesting during his morning subway ride to work. He's drinking less, much less and by the end of January, he's stopped drinking completely.

You Are Here

One evening, the cable goes out and Alex is faced with a night alone and no solace of TV. He thinks about going to a bar he passes on his way to the subway—they have a television—he's seen its glow through the window, but he doesn't want to be tempted by a neat glass of Jack.

He decides to take a walk around the World's Fairgrounds. He hasn't been there before, only looked at it from the window of his room.

It's windy and cold. The park is empty and everything seems rundown and neglected. A stainless-steel sculpture of a rocket ship has a broken fuselage that creaks in the wind and dead weeds poke through cracks in the sidewalks.

This is what they thought the future would look like in 1964, thinks Alex. *This is what they thought the future would look like the year I was born.*

He wanders, his hands deep in the pockets of his jacket, until he sees a dried up fountain circled by benches on boomerang-shaped legs. After staring at the benches for a few moments he sits down on one of them.

He can hear the rush of traffic from the nearby Long Island Expressway, it sounds like a river in a way, one that would never run dry. Every once in a while, a jet headed to or from LaGuardia roars above. When Alex looks up, he can see their shiny bellies.

Suddenly, he feels really good about everything, and finally ready to think about what's happening in his life. He starts thinking about Zoë and meeting her five years ago when she'd come into Penn Books looking for a copy of *Circling the Drain* for the train ride out to Montauk. She'd come back in when she returned to the city and bought *Bad Haircut* and Alex had asked her out for coffee.

They'd talked about books. She'd been impressed that he worked in a bookstore. "And an independent one," she'd said, her green eyes sparkling, but steady. "That must be so interesting."

It was. And it still is—especially now that Alex isn't coming in hungover. There're the regulars even though a Borders opened up above;

and worn-out commuters with time to kill before the LIRR takes them back to the suburbs; and the homeless guy, Frank, who flips through the Zagats at the register and comments about the restaurants as if he's actually eaten in them.

And Alex has health insurance. And he likes the people he works with. They have brilliant conversations when it's slow and they all feel morally superior to anyone who works in the chains where they sell more yoga mats and mocha lattes than actual books.

It then dawns on Alex that coming to New York—with no dreams of *being* anything—that coming to New York just to *be* here—and working at a bookstore in the bowels of the city was OK. There were worse ways to spend his life.

He fingers his cell phone in the pocket of his jacket. What he really wants to do is talk to Zoë, but he doesn't know what to say. He doesn't think she'll be interested in hearing about his epiphany or how TV got him to stop drinking.

Maybe I can just ask her to dinner. I'll tell her everything over risotto at Puttanesca. Or maybe I'll just tell her that I love her and I don't know if I've got my shit together yet, but at least I know where all my shit is.

As he sits there on the bench, trying to figure out what to say, he feels something cold against his temple and somebody behind him says, "Hand over your wallet."

Alex hears the words, but they don't register since he's so lost in thought. "I'm sorry," he says, without moving. "What did you say?"

"I said, 'Give me your wallet or I'll blow your fuckin' brains out.'"

"Oh," says Alex, "I actually don't *own* a wallet. I don't believe in them."

The cold metal digs into his skull. "Just shut up and empty your pockets."

Alex does as he's told and hands three dollars and twenty-one cents over his shoulder.

"That's it? That's all you fuckin' have?"

"Sorry." Alex hears the coins fall and tink onto the pavement.

"Just put your goddamn hands in the air. Stay there and count to a hundred. With your eyes shut."

Alex begins to count and hears the man run off behind him, but keeps counting past one hundred, letting it all sink in. He's a bit shaken, but also thrilled. Getting mugged was another New York experience and it had only cost him three dollars and twenty-one cents. He keeps counting until a plane flies overhead, then he opens his eyes and looks behind him and sees that he's alone in the park again. He turns back to the fountain and sits there with his legs outstretched and his hand around his cell phone, holding it out like a remote control.

Neighbors

The elevator of 80W80 dings open on the 10th floor and Mrs. Zaplinski shuffles out with her walker while Jayne leans against the door to keep it from sliding shut.

"There's that smell again." Mrs. Zaplinski sticks her nose in the air and sniffs. "It's gotten worse, hasn't it?"

"Much worse." Jayne scrunches up her nose and tosses a handful of red hair over her shoulder.

"It's time to get to the bottom of what it is." Mrs. Zaplinski follows her nose and her walker down the hallway. She's actually quite tired from today's outing in the park. Her knees are bothering her; she wants to get back into her apartment and put her feet up, but this stench has been lingering on the 10th floor for nearly a week. "We're going to find out where that damn smell is coming from."

Jayne rushes ahead, sniffing like a setter. "I think it's coming from 10-S," she says.

"Madeleine Crane," says Mrs. Zaplinski. "Her and those damn cats. Probably hasn't changed the litter box." She lowers her voice to a whisper and stops moving. "I think it's disgusting to own a cat. Dogs are one thing. They do their business outside—but cats! And Madeleine has four of them." She begins shuffling down the hall again. "Knock on the door, Jayne."

Jayne knocks.

The door is green. All the doors in the building were painted green when Dewitt Kensington bought the place. He also had the lobby re-done and began raising the rents wherever he could.

Above the peephole of Madeleine's green door, is a plywood wreath with the faces of four white cats and the word 'Welcome' running across the center. It's attached to the door with several pieces of yellowed Scotch tape.

Mrs. Zaplinski lets go of her walker and stands as upright as she can. "Madeleine," she shouts. "You've got to change your litter box. You're sticking up the whole building."

There's no answer. Jayne unzips her jacket.

"Knock again," says Mrs. Zaplinski. "She's probably watching *General Hospital*. Every day at three. The cats watch it too. From the sofa. They line up in a row next to her."

Jayne bangs the door with her fist.

10-E opens and Azazel Braunstein steps out into the hall wearing one of those God-awful sweaters she knits and sells for hundreds of dollars on the internet. Mrs. Zaplinski is convinced that people will buy anything on the internet. Eventually, it'll be the downfall of civilization.

"Azazel," says Mrs. Zaplinski. "Do you smell it?"

Azazel sniffs, then shrugs her shoulders. "My sinuses," she says.

"Well, the hallway reeks and it's coming from Madeleine Crane's apartment."

"I haven't seen her in a while," says Azazel. "Maybe she went to Florida to visit her niece."

"Doesn't she have you take care of her cats when she goes to Florida?" says Mrs. Zaplinski.

"You're right." Azazel lets out a little laugh that sounds like she's trying to clear her sinuses. "I guess she couldn't be away."

"Knock again, Jayne. Azazel, call Stanley, get him up here with the keys."

Azazel goes back into her apartment but leaves the door open and Mrs. Zaplinski can see straight into her pack-ratted kitchen. "Look at that," she says to Jayne, not bothering to whisper. "That apartment is a fire hazard. It's no wonder MacGregor left her." She turns back to Madeleine's door. "Are you in there, Madeleine? Answer the door."

Jayne continues to bang and the cat wreath falls to the floor. Jayne picks it up and hands it to Mrs. Zaplinski. "I hope she's alright," she says.

"I'm sure she's fine." Mrs. Zaplinski looks down at the wreath and runs her fingers over the row of cat heads. "Madeleine's younger than I am." She doesn't have bad knees either, or diabetes. And her mind is sharp.

Azazel comes back in the hall just as Stanley arrives. He tips his doorman's cap as he gets off the elevator. "Mrs. Z," he says. "Jayne. Long time no see. Long time no see." He laughs since they just saw him only moments ago in the lobby. Stanley does not, however, acknowledge Azazel. He doesn't like her, although he's quite chummy with MacGregor who still walks most of the dogs in the building. The two of them are always chitchatting.

Stanley jiggles the key into the lock of 10-S; the door opens and the stench barrels out with such force that it pushes them all backwards.

"Whoa, that's bad," says Stanley. "Really bad." He takes a deep breath, covers his mouth and nose with his palm and rushes in.

Jayne gags, but follows, as does Azazel.

Mrs. Zaplinski remains in the hallway holding the wooden wreath. She pulls a crumbled pink tissue from the pocket of her coat and holds it over her nose.

"Jesus Christ," she hears Stanley say. "Get off of her. Get off. Shoo, shoo."

10-N's door opens and the new tenant pokes his head out. Greg Something-or-Other. According to Stanley, he owns an art gallery in Brooklyn and pays almost $7,000 a month for an apartment identical to Mrs. Zaplinski's, Madeleine's and Azazel's rent controlled one-bedrooms, but with new cabinets and appliances and a lot more outlets.

"Everything OK?" he asks.

"It's Madeleine Crane. Can't you smell it?"

"I thought it was cooking coming from..." He points at Azazel's wide-open door.

Mrs. Zaplinski thinks this is funny, but rather than chuckling, she raises her left eyebrow. "Hmmp," she says.

Azazel comes back out of 10-S gagging, her sinuses apparently cleared. "My God," she says. "The cats."

"What?" says Mrs. Zaplinski. "What happened to Madeleine?"

"She's dead," says Azazel. "In the bathroom. She must've slipped. And the cats. She must've been there for awhile."

Mrs. Zaplinski imagines the look on Dewitt Kensington's face when he hears the news. Stanley will no doubt be the one to tell him. She imagines the contractors coming in with the new cabinets that will be painted white and the new Sub-Zero refrigerator. She wonders how many new outlets will be installed in the living room. She wonders how much the rent will be.

Coats

The subway seat looks clean when Cliff Hobart sits down on it, but when he stands up for his stop on 14th Street, the back of his camelhair coat is almost stuck to it. He makes his way off the train, turns around on the platform and pulls the coat out flat. There on the back of it, is a patch of something clear and shiny, but sticky-looking; like half-dried shellac.

Cliff is repulsed to touch it. *What's clear and sticky and likely to be on a New York City subway seat?* He doesn't want to know.

He drops the coat off at the cleaners on Irving Place and walks to his office with the lapels of his suit pulled up to his ears against the snow and wind.

Unlike many therapists, the walls of Cliff's office are not covered with modern art or primitive African masks. There are no bookshelves of psychology texts; no plants sucking up the sunlight coming through the windows. There're no pillows on the couch. There's nothing in his office to distract his clients from the matter at hand—The Session.

His last client of the day is Tim Sporran, a reporter for the *Post*. He's been anxious lately; it's hard for him to sleep. When he finally does begin to doze, he jerks awake from nightmares about being pushed off a tall building.

After listening to him for forty minutes, Cliff offers his advice: "Go home and clean out your sock drawer."

"My sock drawer?" says Tim.

"Exactly. You don't have any control over your unconscious—none of us does, but you have control over your sock drawer. Throw out all the socks with holes in them and the ones that have lost their mates. You won't miss them, but you'll gain a little more control over your life." Cliff looks at his watch. "Same time next week?" he asks.

"Sure," says Tim.

By the time Cliff leaves his office, the snow has turned to slush. There's now a pathway of soggy, broken-down cardboard boxes leading up to the counter of the dry cleaner where he left his coat. The woman who had been there in the morning brings it out to him sheathed in a plastic bag reading, 'This Is NOT a Toy.'

Cliff turns it around and lifts up the plastic. The clear, sticky patch is now black, hard and puffed up, like a piece of burnt piecrust.

"This is worse than it was before," he says.

"We did what we could." The woman has large rimless glasses that magnify her eyes, making her look like an insect. "Whatever's on there isn't coming out. I'm sorry. We'll only charge you half."

"I'm not paying anything." Cliff throws the coat on the counter. "You're crazy if you think I'm going to pay for that. You can keep the damn thing."

He storms out over the cardboard pathway and hails a cab home.

There's a Post-it from his wife on the dining room table when he gets there. She's had to run over to Bed of Roses, the floral shop she owns; there's chicken in the fridge. The note is signed, 'Love, Gail' and 'love' is underlined twice.

Cliff orders Thai instead and looks out the window while he's on the phone with the restaurant. It's snowing again. The buildings on the other side of 80th Street are fuzzy and blurred in the white gusts that seem to blow in several directions at once. It'll be cold in the morning and he has no coat.

While he waits for his food to come, he pokes around in the hall closet to see if there's anything warm for him to wear. In the very back, is a parka that he wore when he and Gail had rented a cabin in Rockland County on the weekends. *We haven't done that in years,* he thinks. *Funny, she saved this.* The standing rule in the household was if something hadn't been worn in eighteen months, it was donated to the homeless.

Cliff drapes the parka over the back of the sofa and eats his dinner while watching a documentary about the czars of Russia on the History Channel; the snowy, night sky a backdrop through the window behind the TV.

After his meal, he throws the takeout containers into the trash, goes back to the sofa and sits down with the parka folded up on his lap. He starts thinking about the weekends he and Gail had spent in Rockland County. They'd always rented the same cabin from a man named Peters, who was a taxidermist. The cabin had a stuffed moose on the wall over the fireplace and other smaller animals throughout. He and Gail had given them all names. They'd called the moose Marty, but sitting there on the sofa, Cliff can't remember any of the other animals' names.

It suddenly seems very important for him to remember them. He spreads the parka out over his lap. They'd been trying to have a child back then. They were name obsessed.

Was there a stuffed rabbit named Otis? Or was that the name of Gail's Basal thermometer? Everything had a name, and they made love by the clock and by charts and graphs, and Gail would hold her knees up to her chest afterwards, tilting her pelvis to give his sperm an extra advantage while she chanted possible names for a baby they never ended up having.

Charles. Oscar. Maggie. Philip. Elizabeth. Samantha. Alice. Robert. Dawn.

A Pair

One black leather glove, left on the seat of a cab now headed uptown.

    The other glove is snug in the pocket of a Burberry coat, not yet knowing that its mate is lost forever, and its own purposefulness gone with it.

Because it is Bitter, Because it is My Heart

G.E.L. is ridiculously dark—lit only with votive candles in the center of each black marble table and half-moon shaped lamps on the dark red walls—but Lowell had suggested it. Barbara pats his knee as she leans across the table towards her son, Greg and asks, "When is Cassandra getting here? I'm starving."

Joyce Carol Oates is at the table next to them, eating alone. At least it looks like Joyce Carol Oates. Barbara can't tell for sure; it's too dark. Barbara had met her agent once, years ago at the Frankfurt Book Fair, when she'd first started Reid & Co. He'd said she was the perfect client; just spewed out book after book without any pep talks or ego stroking.

Barbara had been envious. Her handful of clients back then had never been able to finish their second book without constant coddling and an occasional visit to Betty Ford. Then she'd found Lowell Farber. Although he only writes two books a year and his name isn't dropped in literary circles—at least there's a fan-club of swooning, middle-aged women devoted to dissecting his novels and *Anna, I'm Calling Collect* had been made into a major motion picture starring Jamie Lee Curtis.

Lowell was such a good client that Barbara had married him.

"It's Candace," says Greg, and finishes his drink. "Not Cassandra."

"Sorry," says Barbara. "Candace." She taps her index finger against her forehead, says the name again, and sneaks another peek at Joyce Carol Oates—she's having wine with her dinner. White wine. The glass is half empty. "What is it about you and women whose names begin with 'c'? Every one of your girlfriends since college had a name that began with 'c.' Caitlin, Colette, Carrie. There *are* twenty-five other letters."

"I never realized that, Mom." Greg presses a button on his watch and the watch glows bright blue in the dark restaurant. "She should be here by now," he says. "Her rehearsal ended at six."

"Nice watch," says Lowell. "May I see it?"

"Candace bought it for me." Greg smiles, unfastens his watch and hands it to Lowell. "Forty bucks on Canal Street."

"She buys knock-offs?" says Barbara. "Doesn't she have any respect for intellectual property? Knock-offs are the same as stealing—plain and simple."

Greg shrugs. A lock of his dark hair slides over one eye, making him look like his father, Barbara's second husband.

"What's the name of the show that Candace is in?" asks Lowell.

Joyce Carol Oates is wiping her plate with a piece of bread. Her skin is luminous and papery, like parchment. She takes tiny bites, chews and swallows, chews and swallows.

"*Breakfast in America.*" Greg rakes his hair back in place, showing the small star-shaped scar on his forehead, the result of falling onto the corner of a coffee table when he was just learning to walk. "It's a musical based on songs by Supertramp."

"Doesn't anybody actually *write* music for Broadway anymore?" Barbara's stomach growls, she opens her menu and holds it near the votive candle to read it.

"Interesting things, knock-offs," says Lowell. "Perhaps I'll use them as an element in my next novel. Maybe the heroine is an undercover cop working on a knock-off Rolex sting." He lights the watch over Barbara's shoulder, illuminating the menu. "Does it keep good time?"

"So far."

Barbara reads the menu and wonders what Joyce Carol Oats ordered. Lowell had said that everything at G.E.L. has gelatin as an ingredient and Joyce Carol Oats is a vegetarian. At least that's what Barbara thinks she heard or read somewhere. She *looks* like a vegetarian. But maybe she's one of those vegetarians who eat chicken and fish and things made from boiled cow hooves. "Why don't you call Candace?"

"I got her voicemail." Greg rattles the ice cubes in his glass. "She's probably on the subway."

Barbara looks up from the menu as their waiter emerges from the darkness and approaches the table for the fifth time since they'd been seated. He looks down at the empty chair. "No sign of the other party yet?" he asks. "Do you want to go ahead and order?"

"I think we should wait." Lowell returns the watch to Greg.

"Just an appetizer," says Barbara. "We'll split it. Why should we suffer just because Candace doesn't believe in being on time?"

"Barbara," says Lowell. "Please."

"No, that's OK," says Greg. "I'm sure she'll be here soon. The Caviar Aspic sounds good."

"You read my mind," says Barbara. "Lowell, what do you say?"

"Fine by me." He orders the aspic and another round of drinks.

Joyce Carol Oates signals the waiter for her check. Her fingernails are very short, as if she bites them. Barbara wonders if the waiter knows who she is. He doesn't seem to.

"So, the gallery." Barbara looks at her own nails, freshly manicured, but in a color she suddenly doesn't like. It's too beige. "It's doing well?"

"Eh. It's all about the Japanese." Greg refastens the watch around his wrist. "They're the only ones I've really sold to."

"It's tough when you first start out," says Barbara. "And with the economy and all…"

"Didn't I read something about one of your artists in the *Times*?" Lowell pushes away from the table and rests his arm on the back of Barbara's chair. "A security guard that paints watercolors?"

"Norm Schumer," says Greg. "I just sold eight of his paintings to the president of Mitsubishi. That was—" Greg's jacket begins to vibrate and he takes his cell phone out from an inside pocket. Like the watch, it glows bright blue in the darkness. "It's Candace," he says. "Excuse me a minute." He answers the phone as he stands and walks towards the door in a blue halo.

The fresh drinks arrive and Joyce Carol Oats gets her check.

"Greg looks tired." Barbara pulls the olive from her martini and bites it off the cocktail stirrer, its flesh squeaks against her teeth. "Don't you think?"

Lowell raises his glass of Scotch to his lips. "He's probably just worried that you're going to be a bitch to Candace."

"Lowell!" A chunk of chewed olive flies from Barbara's mouth and lands on the table. She looks sideways to see if Joyce Carol Oates has noticed, but she's busy scrutinizing the check. Barbara wonders if she'll pay with a credit card. Would her whole name be on the card? Or just J.C. Oates? "Me a bitch?" Barbara says in a low voice. "Please."

"You know what I'm talking about. Barbara. I've been to how many of these little meet-the-'C'-girl dinners since we were married? You always find fault with the girls."

"I do not." She discreetly picks up the chewed olive chunk and deposits it beneath the table.

"Cassie wore too much make-up; Caitlin used the wrong fork for her salad. What's-her-name, the one that worked at FOX News—you made her cry." He swallows a healthy mouthful of Scotch. "I don't know why Greg does this, subjecting his girlfriends to you."

"He trusts my judgment, Lowell." Barbara reaches for her martini. It's cool in her hand, but the glass is sweating and it slips slightly as she lifts it from the table.

"Just try to be nice to Candace when she gets here. Would you do that, please? If she has fake boobs and a fake Prada bag, just keep it to yourself, OK? Greg's thirty-six years old, let him find out what's wrong with his women himself. Like the rest of us do."

Joyce Carol Oates gets up. It is definitely her. She looks directly at Barbara, her parchment face, a tiny moon surrounded by a black mass of hair. Barbara feels her own face flush pink. Joyce Carol Oates turns and leaves, just as Greg comes back to the table and sits down with a sigh.

"Candace's not going to make it," he says. "Something came up."

Barbara doesn't say what she wants to say about Candace's rudeness. She holds her tongue—literally between her teeth. She holds it there until she tastes blood, then takes a sip of her martini. The vodka stings. Barbara winces. "That's too bad," she says, and pats Lowell's knee under the table. "I was really looking forward to meeting her."

Outside the restaurant, Joyce Carol Oates hails a cab uptown.

It's in the Stars

The walls of Krystal's Salon look lavender, but they're actually white. It's just the glow of the purple neon sign in the window. The sign is shaped like a hand; in the center it says 'Spiritual Liaison.' Underneath it is Krystal's phone number.

Krystal sits on a white wicker loveseat looking out at the street through the sign, and eating cut-up pineapple out of a plastic container that she got from the deli. People hurry by on the sidewalk, shoulders pulled up to their ears in the cold, heads ducked from the wind, eyes down, wary of ice.

"I predict," she says aloud to herself and the stars, her mouth full of half-chewed pineapple, "that it'll be slow tonight."

Her phone on the matching white wicker table rings. She finishes chewing the pineapple and swallows before she answers. "Krystal's Salon."

"Krystal, this is Henry."

"Henry! I was just thinking of you."

"You were?"

"Yes." She puts the container of pineapple down on the table and moves the phone onto her lap. It's a rotary phone from the 1980's—white and styled to look antique and French. It glows lavender in the light from the neon as well, so does the wicker furniture and Krystal's skin.

"Not five minutes ago," she says, "I had a vision of you and the numbers 3, 5, 10, 33 and 56. The stars are saying you should play those numbers tonight."

"3, 5, 10, 33 and 56?" says Henry. "That's funny. I went on an interview today at 56 West 33rd Street. On the 10th floor, suite 5. It was at 3PM. I was calling to see if I'm going to get the job."

Krystal scowls at the phone and then looks out onto the street. There's a couple on the corner trying to hail a cab. Their breath puffs out in thick clouds. "Henry," she says, "I told you, it's not the time to look for a new job. Trust me."

"I'm not making any money working on commission," says Henry. "I'm going to have to get a roommate to help with the rent. I'm too old for that. This new job would be straight salary selling beverages to delis. That's a lot easier than selling closet make-over packages for a self-proclaimed self-help guru."

"Forget about it." Krystal flicks at a piece of pineapple caught between her front teeth with her tongue. "Just go play the lottery with 3, 5, 10, 33 and 56. You'll be able to retire with the winnings and you won't ever need to have a roommate. The stars and I say there's big money in your future. Have we ever been wrong?"

Henry sighs on the other end. Krystal can see him nodding his head. "OK," he says, "I'll go play 3, 5, 10, 33 and 56. Thank you, Krystal. I'll mail you an offering in the morning."

Krystal hangs up and looks out at the street. The couple trying to hail a cab is still on the corner, arms raised and frantically waving. "They won't get a cab there," says Krystal. "Not tonight. I see it. They'll get one if they walk over to Broadway."

She watches them in the cold and thinks about poking her head out the door and telling them where to go. Give them a little freebie. This one's on the stars. They might come back another time and turn into regular clients. She and the stars could help them with the problems they're having. They could really use her services.

As she watches them, a girl with long, bright red hair and wearing a long, black wool coat hurries up the stairs and into the salon. A blast of cold, dry air comes in with her. Krystal pulls her shawl up around her shoulders. "C'mon in," she says, "I'm Krystal."

The girl's eyes are tearing from the cold. "I'm looking for Z-Bar," she says. She takes the glove off her right hand, carefully wipes her eyes with the side of her index finger, then looks at her finger for smudges of make-up. "Do you know where it is? They said between Amsterdam and Broadway."

"It's halfway up the block," says Krystal. "It's in the basement. There's a 'Z' over the door."

"Thank you," says the girl. She puts her glove back on and turns to leave.

"You're going there to meet a blind date, aren't you?" says Krystal. "Someone you met on the internet."

The girl turns back, but keeps her gloved hand on the doorknob. "How did you know that?" She looks at the neon sign in the window. "Oh, right. You're a psychic."

Krystal corrects her. "Spiritual liaison."

"Of course. Sorry."

"Don't go on the date," says Krystal. "You won't like him, but you'll try to. He's a jerk. By the end of the evening, you'll be depressed. Don't go."

"Is that the *vibe* you're getting?" The girl laughs and wriggles her palms in the air, fingers splayed. "Is that in my *aura*?"

"Yes, it is."

"Well, I already talked to him a couple of times and he's very nice."

"He's not going to like that you're not a natural redhead." Krystal picks the phone up from her lap and puts it back on the table.

"What's wrong with the fact that I dye my hair?"

"Nothing, but this guy wants a *natural* redhead. He wants the 'carpet to match the drapes.' He's very picky about his women, although he's no winner himself. He's going bald and always wears a baseball cap. Don't bother. He's a waste of your time. Meeting men online is a waste of your time. You should pay more attention to the men that are right around you. Right in front of you."

The girl stares at Krystal for a moment and then says, "I came all the way from Brooklyn tonight. He's a nice guy. I've talked to him on the phone already and I've seen his picture online. And he wasn't wearing a baseball cap."

"It's an old photo," shrugs Krystal. "If you go get back on the 'C' train right now, you'll end up sitting next to a single lawyer who lives in your neighborhood. He's not Mr. Right For You, but you'll go out on a few dates with him and have a nice time."

"Right," says the girl, and smirks. "I'm sure you can see that." She goes out the door and another blast of cold air settles in on the salon.

Krystal watches her walk down the street towards Z-Bar. "That's the problem with giving freebies," she says to the stars. "People don't listen to our advice when it's unsolicited."

She looks out on the corner. The couple trying to hail a cab has gone. They've begun walking to the subway; Krystal can see that. To the 'C' where they'll sit in the same car as the redheaded girl's lawyer that she'll never meet. They're arguing as they walk. About their upcoming wedding, Krystal can see that too. They shouldn't get married. Living together is fine, but actually tying the knot—no. They'll get divorced within a year and hire the lawyer that's on the subway train right now.

Don't Worry About It

Brian and Tyler just make it through the door of the downtown 'A' before it shuts. There're two empty seats. They grab them and slide their knapsacks between their khaki-clad legs.

"That was close," says Tyler. "I thought that cop was going to search our bags."

"So?" says Brian. "You've had your bag searched before."

On the other side of the train, is a woman who's dressed like an Orthodox Jew. Long skirt, clunky shoes, frumpy, body-hiding coat—but she's also wearing make-up, hoop earrings and has a logo-laden Gucci scarf tied over her gray wig-like hair.

"Not when I was…carrying," says Tyler.

"Carrying what? An iPod and a manuscript about the history of salt?"

"And the Post-it Notes." Tyler loosens his tie. "Stolen from work."

"Cops don't care about that shit," says Brian. "They're looking for bombs."

The maybe-Orthodox woman looks up at the mention of the word 'bomb.' She looks at Brian and Tyler's knapsacks, then at their faces and smiles at Brian in a very un-Orthodox way.

"I don't know," says Tyler. "There's the web address on them. And the tag. They look suspicious."

"That's not the kind of suspicious that cops are looking for."

At 14th Street, a blind man gets on. His seeing-eye dog is a black Lab, fresh out of canine puberty, still full of puppy wiggles. The dog zigzags through the car to an empty seat next to the maybe-Orthodox woman, tail wagging, sniffing hello to everyone on the way. The blind man follows in the dog's wake, his white cane tapping. He sits, but the dog remains standing, pink tongue hanging out and flapping.

The maybe-Orthodox woman pats the dog on the head. "What's his name?"

"He's a she," says the blind man. "Her name's Rita."

"Are you a good girl, Rita?" says the woman. She scratches Rita's ear.

Tyler picks up his knapsack from the floor and puts it in his lap.

"Just relax," says Brian.

"I'm fine."

"You look nervous as hell."

"I'm not nervous."

"We wait until Broadway-Nassau. I'll take this side of the train. You take the other. Slap up as many Post-it's as you can. Eye-level. We'll get off at High Street, go to our apartment and smoke the number I've got rolled." Brain pats the pocket of his shirt containing a joint made with pot he bought from a guy who works in the mailroom at Sony.

"What if someone says something?" asks Tyler.

"Give 'em the finger. We're graffiti artists."

"We're white graffiti artists using Post-it Notes with a web address that sells coffee mugs, baseball caps and hoodies."

"We're gonna make a lot of money, Tyler. Stop being so negative."

"I'm not negative. I just don't want to get caught."

"We're not breaking any laws."

"I don't know about that."

At Chambers Street, three middle-aged tourist-ladies wearing blinding white sneakers get on the train. They're debating about where to go for dinner. Olive Garden or John's Pizzeria. They all want Italian. That's been decided.

Tyler takes a stack of Post-its from his knapsack.

"Look at that." Brian peels off the top note and holds it up between the two of them. "A marketing masterpiece. Original street art by B. Cool—the hip-hop rebel from Bed-Sty that spent two years in Riker's for his art. And you can own this artist's work on a lovely, microwave-safe ceramic mug for only $14.95. 'Sip your latte from a piece of New York underground culture.' That was great copy you wrote, Ty."

"Thanks."

"Working in publishing's paid off."

"I guess."

"People are going to see these when they're riding the 'A' tonight. They're gonna think they're cool. They'll take them down, go home, hit our site and buy merch. It'll be hot, Ty. Taki 183 in the internet age."

"The tag *is* pretty awesome. The arrow coming off the 'B' looks really authentic."

"And the bio's amazing," says Brian.

"I like the part about his little sister wanting to go to college and B. Cool raising money for her tuition."

"It's heartwarming."

"Yea."

"So at Broadway-Nassau we do it."

"OK."

Brian slaps the Post-it on to Tyler's forehead. Tyler laughs, peels it off and sticks it back on the stack.

At Broadway-Nassau, a cop with a low-slung German Shepard gets on. The dog eyes Brian and growls.

Brian knows that bomb-sniffing dogs aren't trained to sniff out pot, but wonders if this dog might've worked as a drug-dog before this gig. He picks up his knapsack and puts it in his lap, trying to create a barrier between the dog and the joint in his pocket.

Tyler sits up straight.

"Easy there, Barney," says the cop and yanks the leash.

Barney sees Rita, the seeing-eye dog, and barks. Rita barks back. Barney drags the cop over to her, his tail erect, high in the air. Rita tugs at the harness.

The maybe-Orthodox woman smiles. Brian smiles. Tyler smiles. The whole train smiles.

Barney and Rita touch noses. Ears perked, both tails wagging. The subway goes under the river. The tourist-ladies perceive this and realize they're going in the wrong direction. They begin to twitter. Barney sticks his nose in Rita's ass. Everyone laughs except the cop, the blind man and the now-panicking tourists. Rita likes Barney's nose in her ass and turns to Barney's ass for a sniff. Barney doesn't like this. He bites Rita. Rita yips. Barney growls.

The cop pulls Barney back and apologizes to the blind man. He slaps Barney on the nose. "No," he says.

Barney barks loudly, complaining.

Rita is whimpering. The blind man is yelling about a lawsuit and how the NYPD have turned into fascists. The maybe-Orthodox woman takes the Gucci scarf off her head and holds it over Rita's bloody snout. She's not wearing a wig. Her hair is real.

Shelter

There's a glass of cheap white wine waiting for Kaysee when she arrives at Silk Road Palace. She downs it first, then apologizes for being late.

"We ordered while we were waiting," says Lusa, her voice is slurred; her accent thicker than usual. She kisses Kaysee modestly on the cheek, but with her lips parted. "I got you General Tso's Chicken," she says.

"And we managed to go through quite a bit of wine," says Ben.

"We're flying," says Fig. She sails her hand through the air like a jet. "Vvvroom."

"I'll have to catch up." Kaysee pours herself another glass.

On her salary, Kaysee can afford to drink bottles of Château La Tour Blanche in any restaurant in the city, but she and Lusa prefer coming to Silk Road every Tuesday and getting crocked on endless free Chablis poured from a box and brought to the table in dishwasher-scratched carafes.

She's not, however thrilled with this week's dining companions. Fig Vogal and Ben Bradlee are their neighbors from the 12th floor of 80W80, but Lusa has recently become friendly with them, mostly because of their dog, Mr. Peepers.

Kaysee finishes her second glass of wine in three gulps. "What a day I had," she says.

"What happened?" Lusa refills Kaysee's glass this time and the empty carafes on the table are replaced with full ones by the bus boy.

"Same shit that happens every day," says Kaysee. "The subway was late and crowded—and some idiot was watching the *Today Show* on his iPhone with the volume turned up all the way. There was a huge line at Starbucks and one of those Tribeca über-mommies with an all-terrain baby carriage was having a meltdown because there was no soy milk and then ConEd was jackhammering outside my office. It was so loud I couldn't concentrate. Even though the windows were shut."

"They were doing the same thing outside MyOptics today," says Ben. He reminds Kaysee of a Midwestern version of George Costanza from *Seinfeld*, although Ben is from Connecticut. "Plus, they were using one of those saws that cut into the pavement," he says.

"I hate that sound," says Fig. "It makes me think of a dentist's drill. It puts my teeth on edge. Heh-heh. Get it? Dentist drill? Teeth on edge?"

"Good one," says Ben. They clink glasses and Fig's new engagement ring blings in the florescent lights overhead. The diamond looks odd; as if it feels self-conscious about being on her finger. The two of them shouldn't be getting married. Kaysee considers them a 'crapple'—a crap couple; two people who are marginally tolerable on their own, but absolute shit when they're together.

She drinks another glass of wine and looks behind them through the window onto Amsterdam Avenue. There's a homeless man there, looking into the restaurant. She's seen him in the neighborhood before. He always wears multi-layers of coats—even in the summer. They're always stained. So is his gray beard.

"I finally left my office," she says. "And I headed to the park by the river. Just to get a little peace and quiet. There's gridlock on the street from the ConEd jackhammering and the sidewalks are jammed with fat-assed tourists on their way to gape at Ground Zero or go shopping at Century 21 and one of those car alarms that plays that whole medley of alarms is going off—"

"Oh, yea," says Fig. "I know that one." She imitates it. Loudly. Ben and Lusa laugh, so does Fig. Her chin—which is really more like a fleshy lump that occasionally rises from her neck—wobbles with glee.

"Yea, well, anyway," says Kaysee.

The waiter arrives with the food and the carafes are once again refilled.

"You know what?" says Kaysee. The homeless man has his forehead against the window; it's inches above Fig and Ben. It's as if he's dining with them—only his eyes aren't paying attention to the table. They're fixed on the mirrored wall in the back of the restaurant. "I've to get out of the city. *We* have to get out of the city."

"A vacation?" says Lusa. "Let's go to Texas."

"I mean move."

"Out of New York?" Lusa's wine-flushed cheeks de-flush slightly.

"Yea." The idea has never occurred to Kaysee before this moment, but it seems brilliant as the words tumble from her lips. "Buy a house in New Jersey. In Edison or Montclair. A house with a yard. You could have a garden, Lusa and grow basil and roses and a huge wall of English ivy. And we could get a dog."

"I'd love to have a dog," says Lusa. "We could get a black Lab like Mr. Peepers. We could name him 'Keskiyö.' That's Finnish for 'midnight.'"

"But New Jersey," says Fig, again with the wobbling lump of chin. "Why would you want to live there? Why would *anybody* want to live there?"

"I was born in New Jersey," says Kaysee. "And so was Bruce Springsteen. Besides, if we lived in New Jersey, I could still commute for work."

"But you do public relations for the Mayor of New York," says Ben.

"So what?" says Kaysee.

"You can't do that if you live in New Jersey," he says.

"It's not like I'm a cop or a firefighter—I don't have to live in the city to do my job."

"All right," shrugs Ben. "If you say so."

The homeless man has now wandered off to the bus shelter in front of Silk Road leaving a greasy print of his forehead on the window.

Kaysee looks over at Lusa, but Lusa's staring at Fig's plate. Fig is separating her meal into groups: snow peas here, water chestnuts there, pork in the center not touching the rice. "I'll call a realtor and we'll go look at some houses on Saturday."

"Saturday is my bridal shower," says Fig.

"We can't miss that," says Lusa, without looking up from Fig's plate. "I've never been to an American bridal shower."

"OK, then we'll go on Sunday." Kaysee tosses back another glass of wine. As she swallows, she makes eye contact with the homeless man who's now urinating against the bus shelter. It's a new glass shelter; the ones that they've put up all over the city. On the side is an ad for Snapple—The Best Stuff on Earth.

Things to Do Today

Emily is momentarily dumbstruck when she comes out of the subway station. Right in front of her is Central Park—beautiful Central Park—quite possibly her favorite thing about New York City—even though she's only been in the park once in the almost two weeks she's been living here.

She allows herself to stare at it for a moment then unzips her knapsack and pulls out the spiral notebook containing important information she's gathered about the city and her lists of things to do.

The front page has her master list. Get Job. Get Apartment. Get New York Boyfriend. Get Job is already checked off and today she's determined to Get Apartment (although 'share' was the correct term according to her cousin Simon). Next week, she'll Get New York Boyfriend—hopefully a musician. Someone cute and caring, like Bongo from Shattered Egg, but much younger.

She flips through the notebook to today's list of shares. Yesterday's list had been a washout. It's already been torn from the book, crumbled up and thrown in the trash.

Today's isn't much better. The only place with any possibility is on 23rd Street, which is a plus because she could walk to work and save money on subway fare. It's an OK apartment, but she'd be sleeping on a foldout sofa in the living room of a kinda creepy guy who has a job organizing closets. Emily was sleeping on a foldout sofa now in her cousin Simon's living room for free and Simon's not creepy.

Emily reads the last address of today's list. 80 West 80th St. Apt 10-E. *I like that*, she thinks, *80 West 80th*.

The woman showing the apartment is waiting for Emily when the elevator opens. She has a big halo of frizzy gray hair—like steel wool has been stretched and glued to her head. She's wearing a long, shapeless sweater the color of liverwurst.

"You must be Emily," she says. "I'm Azazel. Come in, come in."

Emily follows Azazel into the apartment and into a large kitchen crammed with mismatched furniture, bulging shopping bags and clear plastic boxes containing colorful balls of yarn. Over the stove, dried herbs hang like slumbering bats. Below them, a pot of something brown bubbles and a teakettle silently steams.

"It's nice to meet you," says Azazel.

"Thank you," is all Emily can manage. She's never seen so much stuff in one room before.

Azazel takes Emily by the arm. "Your email said that you just moved to the city."

"Two weeks ago tomorrow."

"That's so exiting. Do you like it?"

"Love it."

"Good. You've got to love the city in order to put up with the heartbreak." Azazel lets out a sad little laugh that sounds like a Canada goose. "Let me show you the room."

She squeezes sideways by the kitchen table to a door with no doorknob—just a hole where one normally would be—and pushes against the door with her shoulder then ushers Emily into a room so small that the only things that would fit in it would be the bed and dresser that Emily needs to buy. On one wall is a window with plastic duct-taped to the frame.

Azazel walks over to it and carefully pulls the plastic away from the frame. "Come here," she says to Emily. "Come here and stick your head out and look left."

Emily does and there it is—Central Park—right outside what could be her own bedroom window. Beautiful Central Park, where she could take long walks with the boyfriend she'll find next week.

She brings her head back into the room. "I have three written references," she says, "a note from my job verifying employment. And of course, I have my checkbook."

Azazel lets out another Canada goose chuckle and replaces the plastic on the window. "Let's have a cup of tea," she says. "We'll talk."

Emily follows her back out past the kitchen table.

"Sit down," says Azazel. "Tell me about yourself."

And Emily sits. On the kitchen table is a stack of newspapers topped by a sleeping longhaired white cat. There's a fan of mailing envelopes, a small tower of UPS boxes and unopened mail addressed to Knitopia.com, 80 W. 80th St. 10-E.

"Well," says Emily, "I've got a job doing data entry, but I want to get into journalism—that's what my degree's in. I'd like to work at CNN—in the Time Warner Center. I love that building."

"I haven't seen it yet," says Azazel, taking the kettle off the stove. "I don't leave the apartment much. I work at home, knitting sweaters and selling them on the internet. Once in awhile, I'll go visit my sister in Brooklyn, but that's about it." She walks over to the table with two chipped mugs. "I'm out of sugar," she says. "Do you want honey? Soy milk?"

"Oh, no. I drink tea uh…black or whatever it's called without anything in it." She takes a sip. Emily hates tea. It reminds her of being sick in bed as a child. "Wonderful," she says, and puts her mug back down on the clean patch of the table.

The cat awakens, stretches and walks over the obstacle-coursed table and sniffs at Emily's steaming mug.

"Meany." Azazel picks up the cat and sits it down on her own lap. "I hope you like cats," she says to Emily. "I have four of them. Eeny, Meany, Miney and Mo. I adopted them when their owner—the lady who lived next door—died. This is Meany." Azazel takes the cat's paw and waves it. "Say hello, Meany."

"I love cats," Emily lies and scratches Meany's head. "How's it going, baby?"

Azazel lets out a little laugh that sounds like an engine trying to turn over. "I like you, Emily. I think you'll bring a positive energy to the apartment. The room is yours if you want it."

"Really?" says Emily. "Thank you." She wants to say Azazel's name but can't remember how it's pronounced. She takes her checkbook out of her knapsack and writes a check for the first month's and last month's rent, thinking she can deal with the tiny room, the cats and Azazel never leaving the apartment as long as she has that view of Central Park just by sticking her head out the window.

As she hands the check to Azazel, she begins to wonder why the window in the room has plastic duct-taped to it. She makes a mental note to ask Azazel about it one day, but today she doesn't really need to know.

The Progress of Love

Tim can't get over how tall Jayne is. Granted she's wearing heels—her calves are zipped snuggly into pointy-toed black leather boots. He likes that, but she towers above him.

"How tall are you?" he asks.

Jayne looks away from the painting they're standing in front of and down into Tim's eyes.

"Five ten," she says. She has incredible lips, full but not overly so. No lipstick; just bare, slightly pink, very kissable lips.

"In stocking feet?"

"Yea. It says so in my profile."

"I don't remember reading anything about you being tall," says Tim.

"My opening line is: 'Tall, witty faux-redhead seeks taller, non-suit-wearing real New Yorker for pithy conversations over cold beers.'"

"Oh," says Tim.

Jayne flips her thick, wavy hair over her shoulder and the smell of her shampoo floats through the air. It's fruity like ripe, green apples. "Do you have a problem with my height?" she says. "I don't have a problem with yours."

"No. No, not at all." Tim has exaggerated his height on NYLove.com by three inches. He's also lied about living in New York City—although he's at the very first stop on the Path Train and comes to the city every day for work.

They begin walking to the next room. The Frick is crowded today. This week's issue of *Time Out* magazine listed it as a 'romantic, unknown place to take a date'—so besides the usual European tourists in nubby sweaters and overly-thin Upper Eastside matrons, the museum is packed with wandering couples loudly impressing one another with their recently internet-gleaned knowledge about El Grecos, Vermeers and Turners.

Jayne leads Tim into a corner of the Fragonard Room and gestures at the painted panel on the wall. "This is an interesting piece," she says, and reads its title. "*The Lover Crowned.*"

She bends at the waist for a closer look. Tim's head is now above hers.

The painting is of a maiden in a lush, formal garden, coquettishly looking over her shoulder—a virginal blush upon her cheeks. She's holding a crown of flowers above her lover's head, who's at her feet, gazing up at her face in anticipation. Behind them is a cluster of dark trees that almost look like a plume of smoke from a raging fire.

"Very nice," says Tim.

"It's overly romantic and rococo, but there's something about that I like."

Tim leans in closer and inhales the fragrance of Jayne's shampoo.

"By the way," she says without looking away from the painting, "Valerie Chase is my roommate."

Tim bolts up straight. "Valerie?"

"You know, Valerie—the girl you've been going out with for the past four months."

"Right," says Tim. He nods. Not just his head, he nods the entire upper half of his body. "Valerie." Every drop of blood in his veins rushes to his skull, *The Lover Crowned* seesaws in front of him. He clears his throat and looks at Jayne. She's still staring at the painting. "Well," he says.

"Well," Jayne echoes. "Valerie's been talking about you non-stop since you guys met. 'Tim is a reporter for the *Post* and knows everything about New York City. Tim is an amazing cook. Tim plays the harmonica and is a whiz at Sudoku. Tim-this, Tim-that.' When you sent me that email, I went to your profile, read it and it sounded just like the Tim that Valerie was dating. And lo and behold…"

Jayne stands upright. Tim looks up at her. He can see into her nose, it's deep and dark and appears to be endless. "So this whole time that you and I have been emailing and talking, you knew that I knew Valerie?"

"Yes."

"And did Valerie know that you knew?"

"Uh-huh."

Tim churns through the past week in his head. The cool, non-committal phone conversations he had with Valerie, her 'I'm really busy' responses whenever he suggested getting together. "And does Valerie know that you're here now?" he asks.

"She put me up to it actually." Jayne returns her gaze to *The Lover Crowned*.

Tim follows suit. The maiden is no longer looking over her shoulder; she's looking out of the painting and directly at Tim. She's scowling.

Tim closes his eyes tightly, and opens them again. The maiden is still staring stiletto daggers. Her face is bright red. Fire leaps and crackles from the trees in the background. Tim can smell the smoke. Then, with a delicate flick of her wrist, the maiden flings the crown of flowers out of the painting and into the real world. It hits Tim in the middle of his forehead and falls with a rustle of leaves at his feet.

Do You Want to Play Again?

Clenching a Uni-ball Vision Elite between his teeth, Lowell Farber types the first sentence of his twenty-forth novel into his laptop. *The moonlight gently caressed Monica's soft, supple body as Trevor slipped from between her sheets, silently gathered his clothes, and stole away into the night.* Lowell then deals out a game of FreeCell Solitaire to help him think about the second sentence. All the aces are buried; he hits 'new game' until there's at least one ace in the first row.

On his desk, under his elbow, is a yellow legal pad where he's written notes about his novel in black ink; a complete outline of it is written in red. It will be approximately three hundred pages and titled, *All That Glitters.*

Fourteen stories below, in the center of Park Avenue, between the lanes of uptown/downtown traffic is a landscaped median with ever-changing gardens at each end. There are tulips there now. Lowell looks out the window of his study and wonders when they were planted. It's as if they appeared overnight. *What had been there before? Daffodils? Crocuses?* He can't remember.

The object of FreeCell is to make four stacks (called 'cells') of cards (one for each suit: hearts, spades, clubs and diamonds) in order of rank, from ace to king, using the four 'free cells' as placeholders. Lowell vows that the game he's playing now will be his last until he finishes writing the first chapter.

After lunch (grilled cheese and tomato sent up from Euro Diner on 3rd), Lowell's wife, Barbara calls. She's also his agent. "How's the novel?" she asks. "Good, I'm getting a lot done." He moves the queen of diamonds onto the king of clubs, exposing the three of hearts that automatically flies up to its cell. "Do you want to have dinner with Cliff Hobart tonight?" she asks. Cliff is another one of Barbara's clients, a therapist who's written two marginally successful self-help books. He's not a full-time author. "No," says Lowell. "I want to keep working. I'll just have something delivered." He moves the ten of clubs to the jack of diamonds as he says goodbye and hangs up the phone.

Now Lowell is sitting in one of the leather armchairs in his study, with *Gems and Jewels of the World*, a glossy coffee-table book on his lap. He turns the pages, looking for inspiration. Occasionally, he jots something down onto the legal pad. *Early Chinese believed pearls fell from the sky when dragons fought. Emeralds symbolize love and success. The finest quality emeralds are the color of young grass. 'Crystal' is from the Latin 'Kryos' meaning icy cold.*

The background of FreeCell is green to simulate the felt on a card table. When there are no more legal moves, a window pops up telling Lowell he's lost the game and asks if he wants to play again. He clicks 'yes' when this happens.

The next day, Lowell types a few more sentences into his laptop. *Monica always wore her diamond necklace to award ceremonies. It was her lucky piece; thirteen exquisite gems set in platinum. It had been her grandmother's.* He scowls at the screen, then calls his girlfriend. She's moved to LA. "When will I see you again?" she asks. "I don't know," he says. "I'm quite busy. I've just started a new novel."

There's a homeless man lying in the median of Park Avenue, under the mulberry trees. *Is he sleeping? Passed out? Dead?* He's not moving at all. When Lowell looks again an hour later, he's gone.

Every time he writes a book, Lowell says it will be his last. Finishing the book will kill him.

On Tuesday, he tells his wife that he's going to LA. "To do research for the novel. It's set there." "How long will you be gone?" "I don't know. Maybe a few weeks."

In the airport gift shop at JFK, is a display of Lowell's twenty-first novel, *Countless Hours*, just released in mass-market paperback. Lowell stands by the display feigning interest in a teddy bear with the New York Yankees logo on its chest. Perhaps someone will recognize him and ask him to sign a copy. No one does. He buys a package of cinnamon gum and makes his way to the gate.

Lowell does not play FreeCell on his laptop during the flight; he never plays in public. He writes on the plane. Words tumble effortlessly from his brain to his fingertips; the keyboard can barely keep up. The plot thickens. Monica's diamond necklace is stolen. The detective sent from the insurance company turns out to be her former lover. Four new chapters are complete when he lands in LAX.

His girlfriend has lost weight since the last time Lowell saw her; and she's cut her hair. Her face has become a terrible rectangle, with no curves, nothing round. It's the cornerstone to a bank or an office building where nobody likes their job. He only stays in LA for three days. When he returns to New York, the tulips on Park Avenue have been replaced with violas.

After completing Chapter 10, Lowell decides to change Monica's name to Maggie and to make the necklace that Trevor steals from her an emerald one, rather than diamond. Maggie wears emeralds to match her eyes. She is now second generation Irish. Her hair is red, not blonde. He re-titles the book, *Emerald Eyes* and plays FreeCell for a half hour in celebration.

Staring out the window, Lowell images living on the other side of Park Avenue, on the east side, in number 23; a small, brooding building designed by McKim, Mead and White. There's a plaque on it saying it was built in 1891 for a cotton broker turned assemblyman. If Lowell lived there, he'd have a view of the Empire.

It is believed (although not proven) that every game of FreeCell is winnable.

In bed that night, next to his sleeping wife, Lowell thinks about the novel, of the characters, of the plot. *Are there enough twists to keep readers hooked? Enough details about jewels? Do they 'shine' enough?* He closes his eyes and pictures having a book signing in the gift shop at JFK airport. *Why not? No one has ever done that before.* It could happen, Barbara knows the right people. She's a warm, breathing mound beneath the sheets. Lowell cups his hand around her breast. He can feel her heart beating.

Don't Breathe a Word of This to Anyone

Parker gets his chest hair dyed at World of Beauty out in Flushing, Queens where nobody knows him.

The hair on his head is OK; as dark brown as it was the day he graduated from college, but the curly hairs on his chest have begun to turn silver, making him look much older than thirty-five. Getting it waxed is out of the question. It's too painful of a procedure. Besides waxing seems like something reserved for women and gay men. So Parker gets the hair dyed every six weeks.

Today he's arrived for his appointment at World of Beauty early. Maria, who does the dyeing, is still in the back room with another client.

Parker waits out front flipping through a copy of *US* magazine. He secretly likes gossip magazines, more interested in the obsession of gossip than the gossip itself. It too, seems like something reserved for women and gay men. Straight men just aren't concerned with the trivial details of other people's lives.

Across from the waiting area is a woman getting her nails done. Brown. *Odd color choice,* he thinks. *Maybe it's a Queens thing.* The woman is huge. Morbidly obese. And she's on her cell phone—a Blue Tooth. And she's loud.

Parker does his best to ignore her.

"So don't breathe a word of this to anyone," she bellows into the phone. "This is just between you and me—but the goalie for the New York Rangers? They started showing his apartment today. That means his contract isn't getting renewed."

Parker looks up from the article about a generic celebrity's shopping spree in Beverly Hills. The goalie that the woman is talking about lives in Parker's building. He's ridden the elevator with him, Parker getting out on the 5th floor and the goalie going up to the penthouse.

The goalie is a pretty nice guy—he and Parker have talked about the weather and dogs (they both own Labs)—but never about sports. Parker is a baseball and football man, he doesn't follow hockey. He never even acknowledged that he knew who the goalie was or that he was famous— just treated him like anyone else who lived in 80W80.

"Well, they spent all that money on him," the woman continues. She blows on the brown fingernails that are already finished. "And he just didn't perform. I say good riddance. Send him back to Toronto."

She takes a sip from the can of Pepsi on the table in front of her. It has a bendy straw in it. She holds the can carefully so she doesn't smudge the fresh polish.

"He never gave Stanley tickets to any games and Stanley was always moving his car. And do you know what he Stanley tipped at

Christmas? A hundred dollars! Isn't that shameful? He has all that money. Millions! And all he could spare was a measly hundred bucks. And you know, me and Stanley really count on those tips."

Parker feels his face grow hot. The Stanley who the woman's referring to must be the doorman at 80W80. And a hundred dollars was the amount that Parker had tipped him this year as well. And Stanley is a good doorman, an amazing one—but that's what Parker tipped all the doormen and there were five of them, plus the super. And a handful of other people like his housekeeper and his dogwalker. Christmas always puts a dent in Parker's wallet.

Who is this cow to announce in a big, fat loud voice that a hundred dollars isn't an adequate tip?

Parker takes his cell phone from his pocket. He'll call his friend Tim Sporran who's a reporter at the *Post* and, in an equally loud voice tell Tim about the goalie's apartment and contract.

Tim's done Parker quite a few favors throughout the years. He'll appreciate the 'scoop.' And the Blue Tooth meddler will learn a valuable lesson about cell phone etiquette and divulging gossip in public places.

Parker looks up Tim's number and is just about to press 'call' then stops.

Wouldn't calling Tim put Parker in the same category as women and gay men? "Tim, you'll never guess what I just heard." Parker couldn't emasculate himself like that. It's one thing to get your chest hair dyed. It's another thing to get on your cell phone in World of Beauty and broadcast dirt about your own neighbor just to spite someone.

Parker couldn't do that. He texts Tim instead.

Green Tea

From where she sits on her sofa, Zoë can see the fire escape that hangs outside her living room window. It's a small fire escape—not like the ones in movies where brooding musicians can sit comfortably with a guitar and strum through their misery. It's narrow, rusty and it squeaks when the wind blows

On her lap is a stack of stories from her third grade class at the Metropolitan Montessori School that she needs to read. The assignment was to write from the perspective of one of the animals they saw during a field trip to the Bronx Zoo.

She's cupping a mug of green tea in her hands and cradling the phone on her shoulder, her friend Jayne is on the other end.

"I think I need to make some changes in my life," says Jayne.

"Change is good," says Zoë. The story that's on top of the stack—the story Zoë has read and re-read three times now, is by Luke Simpson. His older brother, Craig is in a coma.

"Maybe I should dye my hair back to its natural color," says Jayne. "Or get it cut."

"Uh-huh," says Zoë. Luke's story is from the point of view of a bat named Pete that "hangs upside down in a very dark cave, sleeping deep through the whole day." At dusk when the other bats leave the cave to feed, this bat stays behind. He doesn't wake up.

"Or maybe I should give up internet dating," says Jayne.

Zoë takes a sip from the mug. She doesn't really like green tea, but it came in a tin with Chinese lettering on it and she'd thought it'd make a nice, little welcome-home gift for her husband, Alex. She'd told Alex to move out of their apartment until he stopped drinking and got his shit together. He's sober now, but says he wants to 'stay put' in Queens for a while longer.

"I think giving up internet dating is a great idea," she says to Jayne. "I always think it's a great idea when you suggest it."

Across from the sofa is a wall of overflowing bookshelves. Zoë needs to go through them one of these days and toss some of the books out or donate them to the library. There's a whole row of her textbooks from college, a mish-mashed bunch of mass markets that she'd bought in desperation at airports and of course, every single title that she'd purchased at Penn Books, where Alex works as a clerk. She hasn't been into any bookstore since he left.

"I've rewritten my profile a million times," says Jayne, "but all I meet are these guys that just do not belong in New York City. They should still be in a land with strip malls and cars. Or wherever they come from. Why are so many non-New York guys moving here? Where did all the cool guys go?"

"I have no idea." Zoë looks back at Luke's paper. It would get an 'A' if she taught in a regular school. But there are no grades at the Metropolitan, only comments to encourage self-esteem and a lifelong love of learning, and Zoë does not know what to write. "Brilliant and disturbing. A natural manifestation of what you're going through right now. Sometimes the best way to deal with bad things is through art and the written word."

That doesn't seem right.

Maybe there's a book out there that she could suggest for Luke to read. *Coma: A Healing Journey for Kids*? She'd hate to have to go to Borders or some other chain. It's Saturday. Alex will be at work.

Outside the window, the fire escape squeaks and rattles in a gust of wind.

"I just hate being alone," says Jayne.

Zoë doesn't say anything, but hums her agreement into the phone. She moves the stack of stories from her lap to the coffee table and looks at the fire escape. She wonders if any one who's ever lived in her apartment has ever had to crawl out onto it.

A Day to Remember

The couple has chosen the Weston Pavilion of the Natural History Museum for the reception. Their apartment overlooks it and the huge glass cube of the Rose Center for Earth and Space. The guests will stand beneath the budding ginkgo trees, cocktails in hand and gaze out over the erupting fountains of the Pavilion and view the universe—the solar system actually—nine planets, plus the sun which takes up most of the cube.

Debbie from Blissful Day arrives at the Pavilion while the ceremony is still going on downtown, leaving her two assistants in charge of getting the guests transported from the church via the hired trolleys. She takes her clipboard out of her Blissful Day logo-ed tote bag and looks at The List.

The catering staff, dressed in black uniforms, folds napkins into elaborate origami sculptures. The votive candles are lit, the appetizers are arranged on red platters and the cut limes are tucked into their silver bowls on the bars.

Downstairs, on the door to the Pavilion, is a plastic sign that reads: No Dog's Allowed. If Mr. Peepers could read, the misuse of the apostrophe would bother him—especially since it's on an institution like the Museum. But Mr. Peepers is a dog (and a smart one—the couple adopted him when he didn't quite make the cut at the Guiding Eyes Canine Academy) and he cannot read, so he's led through the door by MacGregor, his dogwalker—oblivious to the bad grammar and to the fact that he's getting special treatment.

At 4:15, the first trolley arrives: a group of the groom's friends from Connecticut and the bride's Aunt Jean. Aunt Jean is one of the few guests not wearing black. She has on a blue sequined dress that she wore to her own daughter's wedding in 1987. The NFL-sized shoulder pads shrink her already tiny body. On her left ankle is a gold chain with a cubic zirconia heart in the center. Its clasp has caused a snag in her pantyhose. She is looking forward to dancing. She's going to kick up her heels and let loose.

Debbie is now in the kitchen looking at the wedding cake. There are paw prints in the frosting. They're supposed to be there, but to Debbie, they look unsanitary.

The band members take their place. The lead singer, a former finalist on *American Idol,* didn't make any connection between the requested songs on the set list. "Can't Take My Eyes Off Of You," "Double Vision," "The First Time Ever I Saw Your Face." She did notice that "We Are Family" wasn't included. Thinking it must be an oversight on the couple's part, she adds it.

Three more trolleys pull in at 4:35. The first contains the youngest bridesmaid, Claudia. She's inherited the Vogal chin—or lack there of. It's really a temporary hill that rises between her neck and mouth when she's nervous or angry. The bride also has it, but is no longer so self-conscious about it. Claudia heads to the bar and orders a cosmopolitan. She's never had one before. Thankfully, the bartender doesn't ask for ID.

In the same trolley are Marshall, the Best Man and his wife, Skye, the Matron of Honor. They resent their positions in the wedding party. True, they were the ones who introduced the couple, but that was nine years ago. They seldom see them anymore. They're not really good friends. Even by New York standards.

Everyone is greeted by Mr. Peepers and MacGregor. MacGregor has been paid $300 to walk Mr. Peepers down the aisle as the couple's ring bearer during the ceremony earlier and to 'handle' him now during cocktails. Mr. Peepers is wearing a red velvet collar and leash with the couple's names spelled out in Swarovski crystals. Between paw-shakings, he tugs towards the fountains of the Pavilion, wanting to attack the water erupting from the pavement. He loves attacking water. The sprinklers in Central Park are his favorites. MacGregor yanks his velvet leash and tells him to behave.

When the couple finally arrives, there's applause and cheers. Mr. Peepers barks and wags his tail proudly. The couple however is not speaking to one another—although nobody knows this but the driver of the trolley. They've had their first married fight on the way over, when the groom sat on the bride's now-crushed bouquet from Bed of Roses. "It's ruined," she'd screamed. "How could you do that? I can't believe you didn't see it!" "If I'd seen it, I wouldn't have sat on it." They smile politely now at their guests and try to look happy.

Appetizers are passed. The shrimp is popular, but nobody eats the sugar cane they're skewered on.

Photos are taken of the bride and the groom and their parents with the fountains and the planets behind them. The rings of Saturn tilt like a jaunty hat over the groom's head, so the photographer has everybody move to their right.

The groom's family paid for the entire wedding. They have all the money and breeding. His ancestors fought in the American Revolution. There's a senator, a congressman and many attorneys. The groom's mother is ecstatic that their only child is finally getting married.

The bride's ancestors emigrated from Germany in the 1880's and settled in the Midwest. They fought locusts and hailstorms. There's a store manager at Home Depot, several insurance salesmen and a few teachers. The bride is the only one that ventured East.

After her third cosmo, Claudia begins flirting with Simon, one of the bride's friends without a date. He works in advertising and is pushing forty. He's flattered by her attentions.

The catering staff ushers the guests inside for dinner. MacGregor hands Mr. Peepers over to the groom and takes his leave. Origami napkins are unfolded onto laps. Wine is poured. Red, white and champagne. Six of the guests requested vegetarian meals. They're brought plates of grilled tofu and Israeli couscous.

The couple dances their first dance. "I Only Have Eyes for You." The bride—in a Vera Wang gown that accentuates her Vogal chin, still in its post-squashed-bouquet-angry-hill state—doesn't look at the groom during the song. She looks over his shoulder at her parents, happily married for forty years—although she's never seen them kiss.

The moon has come out. It hangs smugly above the man-made planets trapped in the glass cube. The lights in the cube have been turned on; it glows purple, like a TV. Debbie hurriedly smokes a cigarette and hides the squished-out butt in the dirt of a ginkgo tree.

Mr. Peepers, with no velvet leash and no MacGregor wanders from table to table, begging. He receives bits of steak, crusts of sourdough bread and a piece of tofu that he spits out.

The Best Man makes his toast. He tells the familiar story of how he and his wife arranged a blind date between the bride (an eyeglass designer) and the groom (an optometrist) and how it was love at first sight. Everyone gets misty. Even Debbie from Blissful Day and the catering staff get tears in their eyes. So does the bride, but she's not ready to forgive the groom for sitting on her bouquet, although he's apologized twice.

Claudia, not used to drinking cosmos throws up in the ladies room sink. Pink chunks of half-digested shrimp splash into her hair. Kaysee, one of the guests who live in the couple's building, finds her and helps her clean up with wet paper towels.

"We Are Family" is played. The dance floor fills. The bride grimaces at the groom. "Why are they playing this?" she says. "We didn't request it." "It's played at every wedding," he replies, "I think it's mandatory." "It's such a cliché." The groom shrugs, stands and holds his hand out to the bride. "Let's dance anyway," he says. "I love you. Forget about the bouquet. Let's have fun at our wedding." "Alright." She smiles at last and joins him.

With all the excitement, no one notices Mr. Peepers slip out an open door to the Pavilion. Free at last, he charges at the spouting water of one of the fountains and bites at it ferociously. His velvet collar gets soaked. He attacks another fountain and another; leaping and turning in circles between each, his wet tail wagging madly. The nine planets plus the sun glow purple in their artificial solar system. The real moon is far overhead in the night sky, no longer visible.

Accommodations

Frank is sleeping in the subway tonight. He's wearing beige pants covered with every stain imaginable. Piss. Shit. Vomit. Turkey gravy from Thanksgiving dinner at the shelter. Mud from when he slept in Central Park and it rained. Blood from getting stabbed in the leg at the other shelter by that nutso-junkie, Lou.

    His jacket is clean though. Spotless. Just like his dreams, that are sparkling white and filled with warm places to sleep; and hot meals are waiting for you when you wake up.

Half Empty/Half Full

Jill, on the verge of fourteen, hates going to the Marymount School on Fifth Avenue. She hates the uniform she has to wear—a tiny, pleated skirt that barely covers her butt. When she walks through Central Park to school each day, she can feel the eyes of the all the creepy perverts crawling up her legs.

She would prefer going to The Metropolitan Montessori School on the Westside where the one-true-love-of-her-life, Craig Simpson went until he was hit by a cab—now he's lying in a coma at New York Presbyterian. Jill is convinced that if she went to Metropolitan, this never would have happened.

Sometimes, Jill also hates her own mother. She hates that she doesn't *do* anything except supervise the servants, take Pilates classes and shop.

Like most girls her age, Jill keeps a journal. She writes in it every morning before school. Today, she writes a hate poem about her mother. She feels guilty as she writes it, but that doesn't stop her. When she's finished, she throws the journal into her knapsack, slings the bag across her shoulder and says goodbye to her little brother, Josh who's eating Cheerios at the dining room table.

Josh hates taking baths, the color green and chicken if he can see the veins or bones. He also hates his new nanny. She has a mustache and calls him 'Jo-Jo.' Josh hates being called 'Jo-Jo.'

"My name is 'Joshua,'" he tells her when she arrives to take him to kindergarten. "My nickname is 'Josh'—not 'Jo-Jo.'"

"But you're my little 'Jo-Jo.'" She kisses him and her mustache hairs poke at his cheek.

"Then I'm going to call you 'motherfucker.'" Josh doesn't know what 'motherfucker' means, but knows it's bad and he likes the way it sounds. "Motherfucker, motherfucker, motherfucker," he chants.

Jacqueline—Jill and Josh's mother—also hates the new nanny, but at least she speaks English. *What happened to all the good Irish nannies? Why are they so impossible to find?*

"Could you please get him to be quiet?" she shouts at the nanny from behind the bathroom door, unable to hear what Josh is actually saying over the shower. "And you better hurry. He'll be late for school."

Jacqueline also hates the extra fifteen pounds that she hasn't been able to lose since Josh's birth. The weight sits solidly on her abdomen and hips like uncarvable marble on an otherwise perfect sculpture.

As she gets out of the shower and dries off, she thinks once again of liposuction, but hates the idea of surgery. She hates doctors and hospitals and scalpels and blood tests.

Maybe I should take two Pilates classes a day instead of one, she thinks and wipes the steam off the mirror. *And no more wine with dinner. Perhaps skip dinner altogether.*

Jacqueline also hates living in the same apartment building that her husband owns. Each time she rides the elevator, she dreads being joined by one of the tenants and she'll have to make small talk about the weather or some other neutral subject.

This morning, the elevator opens on the 8th floor and Gail Hobart gets on. Jacqueline hates her. She owns a floral shop on 79th and when she and her husband first moved into the building, Jacqueline had asked about getting a discount on flowers for the lobby. "Sure," Gail had replied, "if we can get a discount on our rent." The two of them ride to the lobby in silence; eyes locked on the floor numbers above the door.

Jacqueline's husband, Dewitt hates that there are no celebrities living in 80W80. There is the goalie for the New York Rangers—but he's moving out and nobody cares about hockey anyway. Dewitt wants a real star like Bongo or Al Roker. They however, all want to live in brand-name buildings like the San Remo or the Beresford.

Dewitt also hates the Post-it Notes that Jacqueline puts up on the refrigerator. They're color-coded. His are yellow (there're actually, 'canary' according to the Post-it package). Jill's are pink and Josh—who can barely read—has light blue ones. Josh's notes are usually passive-aggressively addressed to his nanny: "Play in the park for at least two hours today." "Wash your hands frequently with anti-bacterial soap." "There are carrot sticks for your afternoon snack."

Leaning against the kitchen counter with a glass of orange juice, Dewitt begins to read his Post-its. He hates the new orange juice—when did 'lots of pulp' become a good thing? After he downs half the glass—trying not to gag as he swallows—Dewitt holds the glass up to the window to look at the pulp. The juice is thick with it—and the glass is spotted. It was washed in a new dishwasher detergent that's organic—using it will help save the planet.

He dumps the rest of the juice in the sink and goes back to his Post-its. One is a reminder about their tickets for tonight's performance of *Breakfast in America* at the Brooks Atkinson Theatre.

Dewitt hates Broadway musicals—especially jukebox ones based on the catalog of a band like Supertramp, but the tickets were a gift from one of their tenants, Greg Palinuck—he's dating the female lead of the show, Candace St. James.

Oh, to get her to move into the building! Candace isn't a superstar, but recognizable in a New York sort of way. She's been on dozens of *Law and Order* episodes, had her own talk show on NY1 and she starred in *Coney Island Goldfish*.

When it first came out, Dewitt hated *Coney Island Goldfish*. He didn't understand it. Nobody did, but everyone went to see it. For months, it was the top subject over cocktails at Z Bar, Sunday afternoon brunches at Good Enough to Eat and chance meetings while picking up the dry cleaning at Aphrodite.

In the most notorious scene—the one that made most people consider the film soft-core porn—Candace lies naked on the black-and-white tiled floor of Bloomingdale's while a goldfish flops between her creamy, pink breasts.

Dewitt is actually looking forward to the show tonight.

The first act of Breakfast in America is disappointing. The entire Kensington family—with the exception of Dewitt—hates it.

"That was so boring," Josh screams as they make their way up the crowded aisle during intermission. He thought a 'Broadway musical' was going to be like a cartoon.

Dewitt lifts him up. "It's not that bad," he says. "And let's not voice our opinions so loudly, OK?"

"It *totally* sucked," says Jill, taking out her phone and turning it on. "It was just these dumb people coming into a dumb diner and singing a bunch of dumb songs. And nobody has a name! It's just The Waitress, The Hippie Chick, The Rich Real Estate Developer. How stupid."

"I actually liked that nobody has names," says Dewitt. "Just titles. That's how we look at people in America. By what they do for a living."

"How profound," says Jacqueline, not bothering to soften her sarcasm.

"What are kippers?" asks Josh.

"They're a type of fish," says Jacqueline. "And they're popular in England." She rummages through her purse and pulls out a package of Tic Tacs. Instead of dinner tonight, she is ingesting a one-and-half calorie breath mint every hour. She shakes out a mint, then offers some to the rest of her family's outstretched palms.

"People really eat kippers for breakfast?" says Josh. "Yuck."

They reach the lobby and Dewitt sets Josh down on his own two legs. "They're a delicacy," he says.

"I hate delicacies." Josh spits out his Tic Tacs; they leave his mouth like a succession of bullets from a machine gun and ricochet across the marble floor. "Can we go home now?" he asks.

"That was very rude," says Dewitt. "And no, we can't go yet. There's still another act."

"Do we have to stay?" Jill rolls her eyes up to the ceiling. "It's so terrible."

"Yes, let's leave," says Jacqueline, holding her Tic Tac under her tongue like a pill, letting it dissolve slowly.

"It might get better," says Dewitt. "Besides, Greg gave us the tickets, it doesn't seem right not to stay for the whole show."

"Greg won't know." Jacqueline puts on her coat, ignoring Dewitt's comment about the possibility that the show will improve. "Greg's not here and his girlfriend—The Waitress—won't notice that our seats are empty." She begins walking towards the doors, Jill and Josh follow.

Dewitt doesn't move. "We're staying for the second act," he says.

Jacqueline, Jill and Josh turn around.

"What did you say?" says Jacqueline.

"I said we're staying."

Jacqueline glares at her husband, then flicks the Tic Tac up from under her tongue and sucks on it hard, pursing her lips.

"The tickets were a gift," says Dewitt. "I don't know if Greg paid for them or got them as comps, but they were a gift. He was trying to be nice and we're going to be nice in return and stay for the whole show and then we're going to go meet Candace when she comes out of the stage door and tell her how much we enjoyed it."

Dewitt plays the whole scene out in his head. Candace—her face freshly scrubbed of her pancake make-up, wearing jeans and a tight *Breakfast in America* T-shirt—poses for photos and signs *Playbills*. "Excuse me, Ms. St. James," Dewitt will say. "We're the Kensingtons." And Candace is instantly charmed by his lovely family as they shower her with compliments about the show. They'll become friends and she'll eventually move to 80W80 —either in with Greg or into her own apartment.

"Why do we have to stay?" Jill asks.

"Why?" Dewitt unbuttons his suit coat and sticks his hand into the pockets of his trousers. He looks at his shoes that he had polished this morning, then looks up. He clears his throat. "Why do we have to stay?" he says again. "Because we, as a family are always looking at the bad side of things—what we don't like. With us it's not 'is the glass half empty or half full,' with us it's 'the water is undrinkable because it came from the tap.'"

"What does that mean?" asks Josh.

"It means," says Dewitt, "that it's time we start looking at the world a little differently. Try to appreciate things more."

"Are you kidding, Dad?" says Jill.

"No, I'm not. We're staying and we're going to like it."

"This is ridiculous," says Jacqueline, but she and the children obediently file back to their seats before the curtain rises again.

In Act II, there's a fight between The Rich Real Estate Developer and the Hitchhiker; The Cook declares his love for The Hippie Chick and Candace has a solo with "Logical Song." The show ends with all the characters in the diner having one last breakfast before the diner is torn down to make room for a high-rise of condos. The entire audience—with the exception of Jacqueline, Jill and Josh—stands and applauds. Jacqueline, Jill and Josh merely stand to leave.

"Well, we all survived, didn't we?" says Dewitt. He begins to help Jacqueline on with her coat. "And it was pretty good."

"It was awful." She pulls the coat out of his hands, puts it on herself as she leads the family up the aisle, the red exit sign beckoning. "Absolutely awful."

"I liked that one song," says Josh. He begins to sing. "Screamer, you're such a silly screamer. Can you put your hands on your head, oh no. Oh no."

"It's 'Dreamer' not 'Screamer,'" says Jill. "I've just wasted two hours of my young life being bored out of my skull. Two hours!" Tomorrow, she'll write another hate poem in her journal. This one will be about her father and she won't feel guilty writing it.

"I could've been home building a Lego city," says Josh. He starts mis-singing "Dreamer" again.

"Stop that," says Jacqueline, she looks over her shoulder at Dewitt. "I may never forgive you for this," she says, "And please don't tell me that we still have go meet Candace. I'll file for divorce if we have to do that."

As he walks up the aisle behind his family, Dewitt wonders if Jacqueline is serious about divorce. *It wouldn't be such a bad thing*, he thinks. *She'd get custody of the kids and probably move to the Eastside, but I'd get them on weekends. I could buy orange juice with no pulp in it and whatever kind of dishwashing detergent I want. There'd be no more Post-its on the fridge. The glass is half full, the water is from a mountain spring and the glass itself is spotless.*

Inhaler

MacGregor gets dressed to meet Jayne by grabbing a T-shirt from the drawer of his dresser. It's a black one from a Franz Ferdinand show—a bit worn, but there're no holes in it, so MacGregor considers it a dress shirt.

He looks at the mirror nailed to the inside of his closet door. He hasn't shaved. His ex-wife, Azazel had hated that—but Jayne had once said that MacGregor's razor stubble 'brought out his peat-colored eyes.' She'd then confessed that she'd never actually seen peat, but imagines it's a deep, rich brown.

The clock radio by his bed announces it's time for Weather on The 10's.

"Fuck. I've gotta get my arse outta here," he says, but continues looking in the mirror as he listens to the forecast. It's 80 degrees now and will stay in the high 70's all night.

"Fuck," he says again. It's too warm to wear a jacket and no jacket means he'll have to carry his inhaler in the front pocket of his jeans.

There's no way MacGregor can leave the apartment without his inhaler. His asthma's never been worse. New York is mad with pollen this year. Each day, as he walks dogs through Central Park, the air seems yellow with it. Most of the time he simply cannot breathe.

When he stops to take a hit off the inhaler, the dogs turn and sit. They look up at him with sad, apologetic eyes, while the cherry trees and crabapples cackle more pink blossoms into the wind.

MacGregor picks up the inhaler from his dresser. "Fuckin' asthma," he says, and shoves it into his pocket. "Even the fuckin' word is for wankers—with that lisp-y lookin' 'th' that you don't even pronounce. Why couldn't they at least spell it 'azma'?"

MacGregor knows that Jayne's aware of his asthma, they've been friends for eight years now, but tonight will be the first night he hangs out with her as an officially single guy with his own apartment.

The plan is for a few quiet pints at the King's Head on 14th Street and then he'll suggest getting something to eat. On the way to Veselka—maybe by the Duane Reade on 2nd Avenue, he'll make his move and kiss her. A long, slow kiss that's been fermenting between the two of them ever since he'd told Jayne about the divorce.

He'll cup her head in his hands, their tongues playfully wrestling like otters, he'll rumpus his fingers through her long hair, their bodies will slam together like magnets—.

"An' then she'll feel the fuckin' deformed prick-like inhaler in my pocket."

MacGregor can make a joke about it. "Is that an inhaler in my pocket or am I just happy to finally be kissing yoo?" And Jayne will laugh—but that moment—that first kiss of what hopefully will be the start of something incredibly fun—will be blasted away by a four-inch piece of olive-green plastic.

Metuchen

"Well," says Kaysee, "in less than twenty-four hours, we'll be in our new home on the other side of that river." She points at the Hudson with her nose, since her arm is draped over the back of the bench and one hand is idly playing with Lusa's blonde hair. Her other hand holds an ice cream bought from Mister Softee on the way over to park.

Kaysee is always eating. She used to smoke—now she eats. Carrot sticks, Pringles, Brach's Butterscotch Discs that she lobs relentlessly around her mouth.

Lusa lights a Marlboro and looks across the dark river where a two-bedroom ranch house with a teak deck is waiting for them. "Metuchen,

New Jersey," she says, exhaling a cloud of smoke. "Incorporated as a borough on March 20, 1900. Population 12,840."

The movers are coming in the morning. Ninety-four cardboard boxes have been packed with seven years of living together in 80W80. Eighteen boxes contain Lusa's papers and books, mostly slim tomes of Finnish poetry and fat ones on New York history. New York is the only American city Lusa has lived in.

Thirty-eight boxes are packed with Kaysee's cooking things. The new house has an enormous kitchen. Her copper-bottom pots will have their own designated cupboard and there'll be plenty of counter space for the food processor, microwave and bread-maker.

The new house also has a garage for Kaysee's car. Kaysee said she'll teach Lusa how to drive. Lusa will have to learn since there're no subways where they're going and walking will be out of the question.

The ninety-four cardboard boxes have been labeled and stacked against the walls. Fig and Ben Bradlee from the eighth floor stopped over earlier with a leather photo album as a housewarming gift. They promised to visit, but Lusa knows they won't. People in Manhattan don't go to New Jersey.

Lusa also knows that she and Kaysee will never come back and sit on this bench in Riverside Park carved with initials and a 'fuck you,' the faded stone and brick apartment buildings of the Upper Westside standing like sentries behind them.

From now on, they'll sit on their teak deck in a yard that actually belongs to them. Manhattan won't be looking over their shoulders anymore. Their own house will be at their backs.

But New York will still be with them, thinks Lusa. It will hold onto them. Tightly. Like a mother's hand you're while crossing the street.

Fingers Crossed

Gail finds it on the floor next to the toilet the morning after the party. A big yawn of an affair that she and her husband, Cliff had thrown for Mark Muller, who'd turned fifty. Mark was Cliff's editor on *Sort It Out: A Therapist's Approach to Getting Clutter Out of Your Home and Out of Your Life*.

Most of the people who'd come to the party were in publishing and they were dull as un-sulfured matchsticks carved from the same piece of bland wood. Their lives were all about their work and that's all they'd talked about. On and on and on.

At one point, Mark had cornered Gail in the kitchen. His breath smelled of sour milk, and he'd told her what he thought was an amusing story about having lunch with a famous writer who Gail had never heard of.

Gail is thinking about the story and Mark's halitosis while she's brushing her teeth the next morning. As she bends over the sink to spit, she sees something glittering from the corner of her eye. Barely visible against the white tile floor is a diamond about the size of a dime. She picks it up and wipes toothpaste foam from her lips with the back of her hand.

The diamond is oval-cut, bright white with no hints of blue or yellow. She holds it up to the light above the sink. "Well," she says aloud. "Who was wearing this last night?" None of the guests had worn anything more remarkable than an Ann Taylor skirt. *So where did this come from?*

The phone rings and Gail slips the diamond into the pocket of her robe and pads into the post-party living room to answer it. The air smells of Mark's breath. The cabbage roses on the piano are already dropping their petals. There's a wine stain on the rug.

"Mrs. Hobart?" asks the voice on the other end. "This is Tyler Daniels, Barbara Reid's assistant."

Barbara is Cliff's agent. Gail had never actually met her before the party. She'd disliked her immediately. Overly-tanned, leathery skin that had been nipped and tucked and Botox-ed to the point that her lipstick-ed mouth resembled a tightly pulled wound that would never heal. She'd come to the party with her third husband, Lowell Farber in tow. He was also one of her clients. And when she'd kissed Cliff hello (a bit too drawn out to be professional), she left behind a long claret clot on his cheek.

"What can I do for you?" Gail fingers the stone in her pocket; she likes the weight of it against her thigh.

"I'm calling on behalf of Barbara," says the assistant. "She wanted to thank you for the party. She had a wonderful time."

"Well, that's so thoughtful of Barbara to have you call. Tell her she's most welcome."

"And she was wondering," the assistant goes on, "if perhaps, you found a diamond in your apartment this morning?"

Gail takes her hand out of her pocket and switches ears on the phone. "Pardon me?"

"A diamond," says the assistant. "Barbara lost the stone from her ring last night and she was wondering if by chance it fell out in your apartment."

"I haven't come across any diamonds," says Gail, "but then again, I haven't been looking for them. The housekeeper is coming at eleven. I'll have her keep an eye out. Why don't you give me your number and I'll call if she finds anything."

The assistant rattles off a few numbers and Gail repeats them back as if she's writing them down. "Fingers crossed," she says before hanging up, then takes the diamond out of her pocket and sits down on the sofa.

The coffee table in front of her is cluttered with crumbled paper napkins, plates of half-eaten birthday cake and empty glasses. One of the glasses has a hemoglobin smear of Barbara's lipstick on the rim. Gail pushes the mess aside, puts her feet on the table and slips the diamond into her mouth. It tastes cold, like a lie, but she likes the flavor. She sucks on it as if it's the sweetest piece of candy she'd ever eaten.

The Secret Goldfish

Luke isn't worried that his mom won't let him keep the goldfish that he's carrying home in a water-filled plastic bag. He's worried she'll be upset that he skipped school, went out to Coney Island alone on the subway and spent $11 to win it playing a game on the boardwalk called Gone Fishin'.

She'll interpret it all as an indication that Luke isn't coping well.

He lifts the bag and looks at the fish. He could've bought a goldfish at Petland for $2, but he'd wanted *this* fish. He'd connected with it as he walked by the booth. It was in the front row of the huge grid of goldfish bowls, and it had seemed to Luke that the fish had been waving to him with its little goldfish fins.

So Luke pulled crumpled dollar bill after crumpled dollar bill from his pocket and smoothed each one out onto the splintering counter of the booth in exchange for three slightly dented ping-pong balls, until one of the balls he threw landed in the fish's bowl.

He slips the plastic bag into the pocket of his corduroy jacket before walking into his apartment building, cradling it so the fish won't get too jiggled.

Stanley, the doorman looks up from the desk and says hello. "How's your brother doing, Luke? How's he doing?"

Luke shrugs without taking his hands from his pockets. "The same I guess."

"Hang in there, kiddo," says Stanley. "Hang in there."

When he gets into the elevator, Luke takes the fish out of his pocket. His mother won't be home yet; she'll still be at the hospital. He'll have time to set the fish up in its bowl and get it settled in a good hiding place.

He knows just the spot.

In the room he shared with his brother, is a bookcase with a fake back on one of the shelves. If you slide it up, there's a space in the wall where Craig had hidden his bong.

After Craig was hit by a cab and everyone thought he was going to die, Luke had taken the bong out, flushed the brown water down the toilet and had thrown the bong out in a garbage can on 86th Street.

Luke takes the fishbowl out of his knapsack and sets it on Craig's dresser. "I've got to give you a name." He cuts the knot off the plastic bag and carefully pours the water and the fish into the bowl. "Something cool," he says, "I'll come up with something."

The fish looks at him, and opens and closes its mouth. Luke sprinkles out some of the fish flakes that the man from the booth in Coney Island had given him. "Take the whole can," he'd said.

You Are Here

"You probably don't have enough money left to buy him food." The fish swims to the top of the bowl and vacuums the flakes into his mouth.

Luke stands on a chair, takes the books off the shelf, slides up the back and sets the fishbowl inside.

"This is going to be your new home," he says. "It's going to be a little dark, but I'll take you out when I go to bed and you can hang out on the windowsill."

He replaces the books, goes out to the kitchen, pours himself a glass of juice and sits down at the computer smooshed into the roll-top desk in the living room.

He'll find a name for the fish by Goggling "coney island goldfish" and seeing what kind of web pages come up. Maybe there'll be something historical or something that has to do with a cool band.

But first, he'll Google his own name. He likes doing that every couple of weeks.

Most of the pages are usually about a black Luke Simpson who's a jazz musician and a Canadian Luke Simpson who's a physics professor. If the safe switch for the internet is off, a couple of porn sites come up. There's a porn star named Luke Simpson. He has a big dick. The only page that comes up relating to Luke Simpson on the Upper Westside of Manhattan is a Lemony Snicket review he'd posted on Amazon two years ago.

Luke has just gotten to the web page to turn the safe switch off when his mom comes in. "Hi, Sweetie." She closes the door behind her by leaning against it.

Luke clicks the web page back to the normal search site. "Hi, Mom."

"I'm afraid we're having Chinese again." She holds up a plastic bag with a yellow happy face on it. "I'm sorry."

"That's OK." Luke gets up and follows her into the kitchen. "Did you get chicken with black bean sauce?"

"Yes." She puts the bag on the table and begins to unpack it. "And I got you an egg roll."

"Cool." Luke opens up the cupboard and gets out two plates. "How's Craig?"

His mom sighs onto a kitchen chair. "I talked to your father today," she says. "We've decided to take Craig off life support."

Luke puts a plate in front of her. "You're gonna pull the plug?"

"Luke."

"That's what they call it."

"I know, but still." She picks a few stray packs of soy sauce from the bottom of the happy face bag, crumples up the bag and tosses it at the garbage can, but misses. "He's not getting any better," she says, "and even if he does come out of the coma, he's suffered a great deal of brain damage."

"He's a vegetable."

"Yes." His mom picks up the bag and sits back down with it. "And Craig wouldn't want to spend the rest of his life like that."

"I know." Luke squeezes a packet of duck sauce onto his plate. "When are you going to do it?"

"Your father's flying in tomorrow. We'll wait until he gets here."

"Is Dad going to stay in the city until Craig dies?"

"We'll see, Sweetie. Sometimes it takes weeks."

"I know." Luke dips his egg roll into the duck sauce. "I read about a guy on the internet that stayed alive for almost six months after they pulled the plug."

"You can come to the hospital tomorrow if you want," says his mom. "I'll write a note to get you out of school."

"That's OK," he says. "I saw Craig just about every day of my life since I was born. I don't want to see him die. I think that's creepy."

Luke takes a big bite of the egg roll. Light brown bits of crust that look like fish flakes crackle over his plate and lap.

His mom hands him a paper napkin. She looks like she's going to say something. Something big and comforting. She doesn't.

Jackpot

It's hot in the subway station. The train is late and the platform is crowded. Simon should've been at work ten minutes ago.

His shirt is stuck to his skin and sweat dribbles down his forehead into his eyes.

He can't wipe it away. He's squashed tight on a bench between a man reading a wide-open section of the *Times* and a fat woman scratching a lotto ticket with the edge of a quarter. With each scratch of the coin, her elbow jabs into Simon's ribs.

In front of him, is a family of tourists from a country where the language involves a lot of phlegm. They're arguing. The mother is pear-shaped, with an enormous knapsack on her shoulders, holding all the things they'll need for a day in the city. Her husband rummages through it.

There's a man with a fanny pack standing by the tracks playing harmonica. He's not looking for money; at least Simon doesn't think so since he's fairly well dressed—except for the fanny pack and he does have a kind of mullet haircut. He just enjoys playing the harmonica on his way to work. Some people whistle, but this guy plays the harmonica. He's not very good. His mouth careens up and down the instrument, sucking and blowing air through the holes. Sucking and blowing, sucking and blowing.

The scratch-off woman has long, shiny nails; painted brown. She probably thinks they look like melted Hershey's Kisses, but they look more like elongated drools of shit.

She checks the numbers on the card with a fecal nail and realizes she didn't win. She sighs, puts the card in her purse and brushes the scratch-off lint from her bellies and thighs. As she moves, Simon can smell the odors fermenting in the crevices of her flesh. She takes out another card and resumes scratching.

Behind the bench, a child screams.

The man with the *Times* begins to cough into the headlines.

An announcement comes on the PA. Most of it is inaudible. The only thing that Simon can make out is, "Thank you for riding the MTA."

He lurches from the bench, hitting the fat woman's elbow. The quarter flies from her fingers and rolls across the platform into the tracks.

"Hey, my quarter," she says.

"Sorry," says Simon, but doesn't mean it.

He stomps down to the very end of the platform, away from the noise and smells, and stands alone by the tiled wall. It's cooler here. Slightly. He un-sticks his shirt from his skin and wipes the sweat off his forehead.

Next to him, a lazy waterbug dines on the wheat-paste left after layers and layers of ads for Hot 97, Steve Madden shoes and the Tribeca Film Festival have been torn down. Maybe he's not lazy, maybe he's dying. He doesn't run when Simon blows on him. Just twitches an antenna like a small, thin arm waving hello. His other antenna doesn't move. Maybe he *is* dying. He's actually quite pretty as far as roaches go. Shiny chocolate-brown, shaped like an almond and smooth as a river rock.

How long will it take him to die? thinks Simon. *How long has he been alive? Has he lived in New York as long as I have?*

Fragaria

Parker is in Amsterdam Deli, looking through fruit salads, trying to find one that's mostly honeydew. The one in his hand is heavy on strawberries—those huge strawberries that are bright red on the outside, but white and tasteless on the inside.

Whatever happened to small, juicy strawberries? he thinks and pushes the plastic container back into the bed of ice with the other salads. The ice feels good on his skin and he tunnels his hand into it.

He hears his name and pulls his hand from the ice, water streams from his fingers. Behind him is a woman with straight blonde hair, cut into a sleek bob. She's wearing black cotton pants and a sports bra filled with grapefruit-sized breasts. A rolled-up yoga mat is tucked under her arm.

"I thought that was you." She has a big voice. Everyone in the deli—the Korean owner at the register, the guy re-stocking the Snapple and Cliff—the therapist that lives in Parker's building—turn and look.

"Hi," says Parker. He knows this woman. He thinks he may have slept with her, but can't remember her name. *Jade? Jennifer? Jonquil?* "How are you?" He wipes his wet hand on the back of his shorts. "You look great."

"Thanks." She smiles. "I'm doing good. Real good. Busy." She lets out an exaggerated sigh. "I just finished a photo shoot for *Elle* and I'm going to L.A. next week for a *Maxim* cover and I just got a callback for a Corona ad.

She's smiles again—a big headshot kind of smile. Her teeth are unnaturally white and even—they look like Chiclets. "But how are you?" she says. "I thought you dropped off the planet. You never called me back about that party at the SoHo Grand. I left all these messages on your cell."

Parker remembers sleeping with her now, but still doesn't remember her name. He met her when Ad Inc did a spot for DKNY legwear. She wore a pair of black stockings for the filming and nothing else. He remembers her apartment was all beige and very neat. He also remembers the squealing sounds she made when she came. "Oh," he says, "I lost my cell phone."

"You lost your cell?" She runs her fingers through her hair; on her wrist is one of those silver bracelets with a heart-shaped charm that says, PLEASE RETURN TO TIFFANY. "You must be catatonic."

"It's somewhere in my apartment, I think. I'll find it eventually. I haven't really looked for it." He picks up a salad with a lot of pineapple, a few pieces of honeydew and virtually no strawberries.

"I'd die without my cell," she says. "Don't you feel cut off from civilization?"

Parker shrugs. "I have a landline, email, a phone at work. I'm still pretty connected." He flips the salad upside down—there's a stripe of bright red on the bottom. He returns it to the ice. "The thing is, I never talked about anything important on my cell. Just these useless conversations I'd have walking down the street with my elbow in the air. 'What ya doing?' 'Nothing. Whaddya doing tonight?' 'I don't know.' 'OK, call me later.' The same conversation everybody has on their cells. It's pretty nice not having one. I actually talk to people now—real conversations."

Her Chiclets smile droops. She looks at her yoga mat, re-tucks it under her arm. "I know what you mean." She looks up. Her face has recovered. She's bubbly again, perky, pretty. Very pretty. "Not having a cell is kind of a Zen experience."

"Exactly," says Parker. "Buddha wouldn't have owned a cell." He picks up another salad. Kiwi and honeydew on top, lots of cantaloupe on the bottom.

"I really just have mine for work," she says. "With modeling, you have to say 'yes' right away."

"Of course."

"You missed a great party. The one at the SoHo Grand. They mentioned it in *New York Magazine*."

Parker nods. He thinks about asking her for her number. He doesn't have it anymore. It was in his cell, never written down and never missed—there were quite a few numbers like that. But here she is, right in front of him and she made that squealing sound when she came. He remembers her riding and squealing on top of him, her breasts bouncing frantically. Then he remembers the breakfast she served him the next morning. Black coffee and a bowl of big, bright red strawberries cut into bite-sized pieces.

He looks at the fruit salad in his hand. There's a slice of red peeking out from under a piece of kiwi. There're probably more strawberries in the middle. All the salads have some. You can't avoid them.

"Well, it was great to see you," he says. "I've actually got to get going." He lifts the fruit salad as if this is his reason for leaving, and in a way, it is. He wants to get home and eat it with his feet propped up on the coffee table. He'll eat the honeydew first, then the pineapple. He'll feed the strawberries to his dog, Buddy.

Think About It

"It'll be great," says Brian. "And you'll save a ton of money."

"I don't know," says Emily, picking at the label of her Sam Adams. "I've never lived with anyone before. I mean, I've never lived with a guy before."

They're sitting in a bar on 48th Street, one with an Irish name that Emily can't pronounce. Brian said it means 'singing and fun.' He is her first New York Boyfriend and although he's not in a band, at least he does own a guitar and can play "World Love" on it—Emily's favorite Shattered Egg song.

"And your apartment's so small," she says. "And what about Tyler?"

"Ty'll be fine with it. It'll mean splitting the rent three ways instead of two without someone sleeping on the sofa."

Brian's wearing his B. Cool baseball cap backwards on his head. He always wears a baseball cap—he has a collection of them hanging on the walls of his bedroom.

"But it's in Brooklyn," says Emily. "I didn't move to New York to live in Brooklyn. I want to live in Manhattan."

"But you're there all the time anyway." He slides his palm onto her thigh and squeezes it. "When was the last time you even slept at your place?"

Emily loves being touched by him; the sudden weight of his hand slipping into the back pocket of her jeans when they're crossing the street, the feel of his fingers brushing hair from her eyes—are almost like sacraments to her.

"Besides," he continues, "you don't make enough to live in Manhattan—at least not on your own. And do you really want to rent a shitty room with plastic taped on the window from another nut-job like Azazel?"

Emily sighs and thinks about the fantasy of her New York Life she'd had when she was still in San Diego: a small, but cute-ly furnished apartment with interesting neighbors who invited her to parties where she met famous people, an exciting, high-paying job at CNN, a fabulous boyfriend who was in a band that played in all the trendy clubs.

"Things just haven't turned out like I planned," she says, and finishes her beer.

"They never do in New York." He kisses her quickly and she feels a tightness in her chest, like a wide rubber band has been wrapped around it. She wonders if he's asking her to move in because he actually loves her or if he just wants her to share the rent. She doesn't want to ask. He'd be honest with his answer.

"Think about it," he says. "It'll be great."

You Are Here

They leave the bar and walk through Times Square. The sun is just beginning to set and the sky is hot pink. It's reflected in the glass of the buildings, making them as brilliant as the lit-up billboards.

Brain turns his baseball cap around so the brim is the front. "You could move in this weekend. My buddy Sean has a van."

"I just don't know."

"Think about it. Really."

On the corner of Broadway and 45th Street, a crowd has formed around a couple dancing to a fuzzy tango blaring from a boom-box on the sidewalk. The man is wearing a tux and the woman has on a long, sequin dress with a slit on each side. It slides away from her legs as she moves. They hold each other close, the man's hand firmly pressed against her back, just beneath her wavy mass of black hair. His face is flushed, his lips whisper into the woman's ear.

"I hate this guy," says Brian, as they push through the crowd.

"'This guy'?" Emily looks closer. The couple spins and dips and turns and she suddenly sees that the woman the man is dancing with isn't a woman at all. It's just a life-sized stuffed doll with a wig. Its feet are tied to the man's feet, so that every step he takes, the doll takes as well.

"Huh," she says.

"I used to see him all the time in the 14th Street subway station when I first moved here," says Brian. "He's so stupid. He's even worse than the Naked Cowboy."

"Let's stop," says Emily. "I want to watch. Just for a second."

"OK. Sure. I guess he's sorta cool the first time you see him."

Emily studies the doll each time the man twirls it close. It has a painted set of large, red lips and long, straight lines for eyelashes. One of its arms is around the man's waist, its hand attached to his back. *With Velcro*, she thinks.

She feels duped and wonders what the man was whispering in the doll's ear. He'd looked so affectionate. She wonders if sometimes he has

171

whole conversations with it, at home when he's counting out the money from the white bucket labeled 'Tips.' "We did good today, Baby. Over $150. We both deserve a day off." Does he sleep with it? Does it have a closet full of clothes?

"You're right," says Emily. "This is stupid."

"C'mon. Let's head to my place." Brian curls his arm around Emily's waist and the rubber-band tightness returns to her chest. "We can figure out where to put your stuff."

He steers her away from the man and the doll, his hand firm against the small of her back and she lets him lead her down the sidewalk towards the subway.

Change

The doorbell rings and Donna hopes it's the pizzas. She's hungry. Being a millionaire gives her an appetite. She scoops a handful of M&M's from the bowl on the end table next to her and pours them into her mouth.

"Could you get that, Dee?" she says through a chocolaty mosaic of colored candy shells. "I simply can't get out of this chair. I'm exhausted. If it's the pizzas, my purse is in the bedroom. Give the guy a really good tip."

She turns to her husband, sitting on the sofa with their next-door neighbor, Leon and Leon's boarder, Alex. Seems like the whole neighborhood is in their house tonight. Norm and Rose Schumer who live up the block, never-married Regina Williams and her three kids, the Wieners and Benji Hart, who at thirty-seven, still lives with his parents.

Donna's whole family is here too—including her aunt Theresa who never leaves Sheepshead Bay unless somebody gets married or dies.

"Stanley," Donna says to her husband, "would you get me some more Pepsi?"

"Coming right up, Baby-cakes," he says as Donna hands him her empty plastic cup. "Coming right up. Anybody else wants anything? Anybody else?"

"I could use another beer," says Aunt Theresa. "Amstel Light."

"Nothing for me," says Leon. "I gotta drive." He's dressed in his bus driver's uniform. His shift starts at nine.

"I'll have a glass of water," says Alex.

"Hawaiian Punch please," says Emir. He runs the newsstand in the 59th Street subway station. He looks different not standing behind the counter of magazines and candy bars. He's much taller.

"Bring a fresh bag of chips while you're up," says Donna, taking another handful of M&M's. "Sour cream and onion."

Her sister, Dee comes back down the long hallway from the front door. "It's another reporter," she says. "From the *Post*. Should I let him in? There's a photographer too."

"Sure." Donna pulls the lever of the La-Z-Boy down and pushes her butt backwards so the chair moves into the upright position. "Must be a slow news day."

Everyone in the living room laughs.

Donna slides her index finger over her teeth, collecting blobs of chocolate and bits of colored shell, then sucks her finger clean. She fluffs her hair and smoothes her T-shirt down over her belly.

The reporter and photographer are both dressed in black.

"I'm Tim Sporran," says the shorter one. He doesn't introduce the photographer, who has a large camera around his neck "Congratulations on winning the Mega Millions," says Tim. "You must be pretty happy."

"I'll say," says Donna. Everyone in the room cheers. Donna wiggles her hips and sits up a little straighter in the La-Z-Boy. "Funny thing is," she says, "I've never played Mega Millions in my life. "

"Really?" Tim unzips his leather fanny pack and pulls out a pen and a small spiral notebook.

The photographer lifts his camera and snaps a photo just as Donna brings her fist to her lips to stifle a burp. The flash of the camera momentarily blinds her.

"Yep," she says, and rubs her eyes. "I'm a scratch-off girl actually. Have been for the past seven years. Stanley bought me my first scratch-off on my birthday. I won a hundred dollars."

Donna smiles at Stanley as he brings in a tray-full of beverages; there's a bag of chips tucked under his arm. He smiles back. Donna wonders if they'll 'do it' tonight.

Another photo is snapped as Donna lifts her cup of Pepsi from the tray—again she's blinded by the flash. When she opens her eyes, tiny red spots swirl in front of her for a second or two.

"Now, I buy ten dollars worth of scratch-offs every morning at the newsstand in the 59th Street subway station and I scratch them off on my way to work."

"That's my newsstand," says Emir. "We sell the *New York Post*. Also Snapple, aspirin and *Playboy* magazine."

"Can I get either of you guys something to drink?" Stanley asks. "Something to drink? We've got Sprite, Hawaiian Punch, Amstel Light, Budweiser and O'Doul's."

"And Pepsi," says Donna.

"We're out of Pepsi," says Stanley.

"Oh," says Donna. "Well, there's also snacks. Help yourself."

"I'm fine," says the photographer. "Thanks."

"I'll have a Bud," says Tim.

Stanley goes back into the kitchen.

"So what made you play Mega Millions after all those years of scratch-offs?"

"That's kinda a funny story," says Donna. She looks at her nails. They're painted the exact color of Hershey's Kisses. It looks like there's a bit of chocolate on her index nail from cleaning the M&M's off her teeth, but when she sucks on it, it's just a bubble in the polish.

"Let's hear it," says Tim, his pen is poised over the notebook, at the ready.

"Well," says Donna, "I was sitting on the bench at 59th Street waiting for the train and scratching my cards. I'd already won $20 on one of them. The train was late. Police investigation somewhere. Somebody probably left their knapsack on a train and they had to call in the whole bomb squad to investigate. I hate when that happens, but what can you do? So, I'm scratching off with my lucky quarter. It has red paint on it. You know the kind they use in laundromats?"

"I was the one that gave it to her," says Emir. "As change. Every morning she gets ten dollars of cards from my newsstand, a Snapple and a 5th Avenue candy bar. I gave her the quarter as change."

The photographer and Tim look over at Emir, then back at Donna. She looks down on the bowl of M&M's, plucks a single yellow one from the top of the heap and puts it in her mouth, but doesn't chew it. She sucks on it and she can taste the yellow of the candy shell.

"Anyway," she says. "I was in the middle of scratching when this guy sitting next to me leaps up and hits my elbow. My quarter flies outta my hand, lands on the platform and rolls right onto the track."

"Your lucky quarter?' says Tim.

Stanley hands him a can of beer. He's wearing the trousers of his doorman's uniform. The elastic of his Fruit of the Looms peeks out over the waistband. Maybe she'll wear her pink nightie to bed tonight.

"I thought about going to the token booth," she says, "and seeing if someone could get it for me, but what are the chances of that?"

"You know the MTA." Leon laughs and pats the patch on the chest of his uniform.

"So I have two more tickets to scratch and no coins to scratch them with. I don't want to use my nails." She holds up her left hand. Her wedding band is sausage-ed into the flesh of her ring finger.

"So I get up off the bench, go back to Emir's, cash in my winning ticket and figure I'll buy something, so I can get change to scratch with. But something tells me to do something different. Did you ever get that feeling in your life? That if you just do one thing that's out of the ordinary, just one tiny thing—it'll change everything."

Tim and the photographer nod, as does everyone else in the living room. Leon lifts a sour cream and onion chip from the bowl on the coffee table. Donna can hear it crunch between his teeth.

"I'm a big believer in fate," she says. "That's how I met Stanley." She smiles at him on the sofa and takes his hand. "But that's a different story." She laughs. "Anyway, I decide to give Mega Millions a shot. And I use the numbers of Stanley and my first date—1, 9—our anniversary—10, 23 and my age, 48."

"You don't look 48," says Tim.

"Thank you," says Donna. She blushes.

"So now that you've won 57 million dollars, what are you going to do?"

"Everything," says Donna. "We're going to buy a new house with a pool, a new car—"

"And season tickets for the Mets," says Stanley. "Gotta get Mets tickets. Maybe buy the whole team. The whole damn team."

"And we're going to take a trip too," says Donna. "Somewhere exotic. Like Tahiti. Or the Caribbean."

"And we're gonna quit our jobs and retire," says Stanley. "It's definitely time to retire."

"Everything will change in our lives," says Donna and squeezes Stanley's hand. She *will* wear the pink nightie tonight and light the scented candles by their bed. She'll also get her stomach stapled and have the fat sucked out of her butt and thighs. "Everything will be different from now on."